Scorned by Hell

KERRY KELLER

About the Author

Kerry Keller has an addiction to caffeine, swearing, sarcasm, and has no filter when talking in public. As an avid reader to escape the drama the world throws at us, she finally got the bug to write a story she would love to read herself.

When not writing books, you can find her working in women's health care, in college, or being a single mother to a very sarcastic pre-teen boy. She swears she's a bad influence to him, so if you cross paths in the future with him... #sorrynotsorry.

Stalk Me.
It'll be a blast!

Come join the reader group to talk about the world of Purgatory Prep, get sneak peeks, and see what's to come next.

Lynx's Minxes-KK's Reading Group
Join my newsletter for teasers and updates
Instagram
TikTok
Goodreads
Bookbub

Cover by: Leanne Brown at Sirenic Creations

Formatting by: Yours Truly-KK

Developmental Editing: Cassie Hurst with Inked Imagination Services

Editing by: Kellie from CreativeLee

Proofreader: Jillian of Locke & Key Proofreading Services

For the family we choose outside of blood.

Trigger Warnings

This is a prequel that fits between books 2 and 3 of the Purgatory Prep series if you want the full effect. You'll find Demons, other magical beings, and sexual situations. This is a darker read and recommended for 18+.

This book contains torture and a traumatic birth story (but no child death).

Contents

Prologue

Lilith

The screams flowing out of Adam are music to my ears. I once thought it was a curse that I couldn't escape, the man I was given to. The Bible had it all wrong. It wasn't Adam and Eve, that sniveling banshee. Yeah, you read that.

She's a damn banshee, always crying about something. Yes, death happens, but apparently not for dear old Adam. God has a sick sense of humor when he paired us up. The first human and the first Demon. Granted, he never thought it would change Adam's soul into an eternal one when I took his innocence.

Even with him being my first, I knew he sucked in bed, just lying there weeping at the beauty of it all. Really? He deserved Eve. When I left, I gave God the finger and convinced a few angels to follow me to the depths of Hell and the bliss it could provide. God decided to create Eve to keep Adam in line and give him a wet hole to occupy his time. Obviously, she wasn't me and she didn't have a backbone, but they deserved each other. Spewing her lies about me is what got Lucifer's, my bestie, attention. It's never a good thing to paint a target on your back when it comes to the ultimate trickster. Even today, her fall from God's grace is still Lucifer's ultimate trophy. That's probably the only part the Bible got right, him tricking her, but I understand why they glossed over that debacle. It's a fucked up story, and it doesn't even have me in it! Who leaves out the main character? Definitely not the book for me, but for those that love it, good for you.

"Lilith. Please," Adam cries out, and it brings a cruel smile to my lips.

Oh wait...I'm getting ahead of myself, let me explain.

CHAPTER 1

Deep Dicking

Lilith

Rolling over in bed, I allow the sheet to fall off my body as I prop myself up on my elbow and take in the erotic sight before me. I watch as my lovers tag-team an apparition I conjured. A firm, masculine ass pumps away into my shadowy figure's wet heat as she's bent over and takes my other lover's massive cock down her throat. He might not look it with his nerdy demeanor and off-putting social queues, but Carl Steinbeck has the stamina of a wild tiger in bed. He's my favorite, well, at least for today. His prize for outdoing the others in our little oral game was this little setup that he allowed Jessup to join in. I loved these types of prizes because they allowed me to recover from my greedy lovers, and I loved to watch them tear apart my apparition. It would be different if it was a real woman, but since it's conjured from my mind, she doesn't have feelings or thoughts of her own; therefore, no reason to be jealous. Instead I can marvel at their physiques. My other two are on clean-up and snack duty. A girl has to eat.

"They're still going at it?" Mattie says, rolling his eyes and pushing his hair back out of his face. Wheeling in the cart filled with snacks in all his naked glory, he gives me a questioning look. Matthew Caldron is my sensitive Mage that has some affinity with emotions. He's indispensable when attending meetings where I need to assess a room. He can read people's feelings and know how they feel, which always plays to my benefit. The place he really excels at though is right here in the bedroom between my thighs.

"That is why he's my favorite today," I say, giving him a coy smile and sparking that competitive streak he has.

"He's only the favorite because you distracted me and I lost my momentum for a second," my brooding Vampire says. Talk about ambition, that comes in spades with Daniel Abernathy. Walking in with a warm washcloth and lavender oil from my bathroom, his shorts hang dangerously low on his hips. I don't understand why he even tries to wear them; he never stays in them long enough between sessions. He's insatiable and correct in his statement. I love throwing him off guard. The incident he's talking about was my tail playing peek-a-boo with his ass. Don't look at me like that. It was funny. All I was trying to do was loosen up the stick that's stuck up there.

"You're just a sore loser, Abernathy," Jessup grunts out. His hips take on a punishing rhythm as he works himself into a fucking frenzy, allowing his Shifter to rise to the surface. Grabbing the phantom's head, holding her still, he roars his release as he slams into her mouth, pumping his hot cum down her throat. I watch in fascination as she tries to swallow it all, but it dribbles down her chin. I know for a fact it's a lot, and his bruising strength surpasses most Shifters. Just thinking about how I had him a few moments ago has me licking my lips.

Yum.

"You keep licking your lips like that and I'll have to fill

them," my dirty little mage says, fisting his cock. I give him a sultry look, and that's all he needs before he attacks. Mattie crawls up on the bed, flips me onto my back, and spreads my legs wide. He runs a hand down the length of my tail, causing me to purr in delight. My tail has a straight nerve ending to my clit and makes goosebumps pebble along my skin as he strokes it like he would his own cock. My nipples instantly go taut as it takes everything in me to hold still and not jump him! Whispering the words to tie my hands to the hook on the headboard, he lines himself up and looks back to Daniel. "You coming?" he asks with a smirk and slams himself balls deep into my dripping heat. A scream rips out of me from his blissful intrusion, but damn, it's a sweet kind of torture.

Pleasure rocks through my body as I adjust to his size. Thank Satan and all his glory since we've been at this sexathon for a few hours or else he really could have torn me open with the force of his impalement. Reaching down, he rubs my clit and wetness seeps out of me as pleasure engulfs my body. I purr for him like a content, fat cat while fire deliciously races up my spine and connects to my nipples, instantly pebbling them again. Pulling my right leg up and over his shoulder, Mattie starts pounding deeper into my wet pussy. His moans mirror mine as our breathing increases from his wild thrusts.

My stoic Vampire swaggers over and slowly lowers his shorts, letting his cock spring free. Wrapping his hands around the girth, he pumps his cock up and down, slowly torturing me. He knows I love tasting him, feeling his hard velvety shaft slide along my tongue, and his veiny cock swells with his movements. He grabs my jaw and slowly runs his fingers along my swollen lips before he brings his mushroom head before them. Opening my mouth, I stick out my tongue to taste the salty precum pearling at his tip, but he moves away at the last second before I can get my prize.

Bastard!

Without thinking, my tail whips out and slaps his ass, causing him to hiss with pain. *Ha! Serves you right.*

He gives me a saucy wink and teases me one more time, but this time, he catches my tail and gives it a stroke. Electricity zips up my spine, making my nipples harder and flooding my pussy, making it wetter. Our bodies now make a wet suctioning sound when Mattie bottoms out with each downward stroke. His deep dicking momentarily makes me forget about the cock I'm trying to suck until I see it in my face once again. I'm about to snap at Daniel when Mattie does it for me.

"If you don't shove that cock down her throat, Danny, I'm sure Carl will," he grunts out and swivels his hips, grazing my G-spot with each delicious stroke.

I let out an unladylike groan, and Daniel slides his dick into my mouth, promptly shutting me up. I suck, lick, and feast on him like my life depends on it, tasting his salty sweetness. I look up and watch his eyes roll back into his head as he rocks into me. Smiling around his cock, gratification rolls over me, knowing I'm the cause of his pleasure. A tongue swirls around my nipple, and the sharp bite makes me gasp, which Daniel takes the opportunity to slam the back of my throat. It's a good thing I lost my gag reflex years ago because he would have destroyed it right then with how forceful he was. Tears brim behind my eyes, but he knows I secretly love it. Carl is latched onto my left nipple like a damn barnacle, worshiping it like my body demands.

Jessup stalks over and roughly pulls Daniel out of my mouth and slams his lips to mine in a bruising kiss, not caring that they were just wrapped around a cock.

"I'm going to the office to wrap up loose ends," he growls out. He pulls away, leaving me breathless but not dickless as he shoves my head back onto Daniel's long, hard, waiting member. He gives me one last longing look, promising more later, before he picks up his clothes and walks out of the room.

Daniel continues to punish my mouth as Mattie swivels his hips to hit my G-spot, making me see stars. Carl worships my breasts by lavishing them with attention, licking, sucking, and nipping at them. All of it is overwhelmingly perfect, and I feel myself closing in on my paradise.

"She's close," Mattie says in warning, increasing his punishing thrusts. Someone pinches my clit, and I see fireworks as my orgasm explodes inside of me. Shockwaves rock my body and trigger Mattie's release as he slams into me one last time, holding me close as he fills my cunt with his cum. Daniel pulls out in time to spray his white-hot cum over my chest and inadvertently comes on Carl as he's still swiping his tongue over my chest.

"What the hell, man!" Carl yells and surges up in anger.

Well, there goes my euphoric afterglow.

"Boys! Let's not fight," I purr out. Satan, I feel like melted chocolate and don't want to move. "Mattie, do you mind cleaning us?" I plead and bat my long lashes at him.

"Sure, sweetie. Anything for you," he says with a wink. He whispers some words that clean us up and releases my hands from their restraints. After everything, I'm picked up and moved to the center of the bed, and my men curl up around me for a short cuddle session.

"Are you excited about going back to Earth tomorrow?" Carl asks, playing with my hair.

"Mmmhmm. I can't wait to start a different chapter with all of you," I say as my eyes slowly close on their own—what a way to start the day.

CHAPTER 2
Backstabbers

Lilith

Waking up in an empty bed, I feel refreshed and energized from my fuck fest and little nap. I crawl out of bed and see a note on the tray with fresh fruit. Aww. They do care! It's incredible to think of how long we've been together, yet they still treat me like when we were first dating. That is the key to a working relationship, folks. That and lots and lots of sex! Happy wife, happy life! Granted, we haven't made anything official even though we've all been together for at least a couple of hundred years now. The mate marks have proven we are meant to be. The four starbursts at the base of my tail are the guys' version of a wedding ring on me, but I want something more. Some of us are coming up on a thousand years of blissfulness. Which is just a drop in the ocean for me, but more than a lifetime for most of them. None of my past relationships have ever lasted anywhere close to what I've experienced with my men now, and I don't see myself trading them in...ever! So, we decided to have a human wedding once we get to Earth.

Dearest Lil,
We cannot wait to see you tonight. Enjoy your fruit. Don't forget to stop by your studio and get your dress, and we will see you later this evening. We'll bring food, no cooking for you tonight. We want to spoil you.
Love- Carl, Daniel, Matthew, & Jessup.

They are so sweet. I don't know what I would do without my men. I'm lucky to have found them at the school when I did. It seemed like every time I had been asked to fill in or come by, I met one of them. While getting ready, I let my mind drift back to how they came to be.

Carl Steinbeck was the first one to join my little harem. Though, back in the 1200s it wasn't a harem to begin with. He walked into my lab class that day with bright eyes, a shy smile, and a mind to rival my own. The Fae weren't known for their love of science, so to find one walking into my class as an elective blew my mind. Who was this Fae that wanted to turn away from his heritage to learn something that I loved? The combination of science and magic was a passion of mine, along with fashion. I know I'm a conundrum, yet I'm an original. I've been alive since the beginning of time.

His tall and lanky stature is what originally drew my attention. He didn't walk like most of my students, scurrying into my room. He walked with his head held high, full of black wavy locks cropped close on the sides, showing off his long ears. That alone drew my attention to him since the Fae back then all wore their hair long and in intricate braids. His long legs, wrapped in leathers, took a leisurely pace as he looked around the room and took in everything with calculating chocolate-brown eyes. They sparkled when they passed over me and landed on the equation on the board.

The school needed someone to cover the lesson in the small class since the previous instructor was missing, more than likely the Withering Sulks claimed its latest victim. I was still in the realm, so I said yes when they asked. I might have exercised my teacher's right and kept young Carl behind to 'play.' Yes, you may keep your mind in the gutter. It was his mind that I was attracted to first, but his body is what made me an addict. Girls, a word of advice, don't turn your back on the nerds. They like to study, and boy, do they enjoy practicing.

Next up was Daniel Abernathy, my cocky Vampire! If I didn't know better, I would have guessed he was an Incubus with all of his swagger. I was sitting at my special table at Darkest Desires Tavern sipping my fairy wine when Daniel came into the picture. He walked straight over, evading the bouncer that was watching the roped-off section like it was nothing. He reached my booth, extended his hand, and said, "I already know the answer, so why don't you just put down your drink and come have dinner with me? I'm the only thing you need tonight, and who knows, afterward...I might just keep you."

I looked up into those hypnotic yellow eyes of his and smiled. He was dressed in a fitted, green linen shirt with a low neckline, showing off the porcelain skin of his pecs. His black hose formed to his toned thighs and when I looked down, I couldn't help but be impressed with how shiny his boots were. He was a sharply dressed man back in the early 1400s and still is today. Now, if he would have only shaved off the scruff around his jaw and thrown away the homemade toothpick that was hanging out of his mouth, he would be perfect, but I was up for a challenge.

Obviously, it worked, but I was the one who decided to

keep him around. He fit seamlessly with Carl and me. He laughed, joked, and gave us the comic relief that we needed in our life.

Roughly two hundred years later in the mid 1600's, I had to shake it all up and bring home my Mage, Matthew. I was working in the office when Mr. Caldron was called in for fighting. He walked in with his head held high, wearing a deviant expression with fire in his hazel eyes. If I would have seen his six-foot-one frame in the hallways, I wouldn't have looked twice at him. His tall and lithe body barely looked like it would hold him up, let alone start a fight. Though, he wore the evidence of being in one. His hair was disheveled from his leather tie, his shirt and pants were ripped and muddied, and his knuckles had some blood on them.

Apparently, he punched another student in the face without any provocation, or so it seemed at the time. I was the lucky one that got to sort out the mess, and it turned out my sweet Matthew was just channeling someone's feelings, and he attacked. It's not unheard of for some empaths to feel someone's emotions strongly, but to be able to be overcome by it within seconds and physically act on it? He was extraordinary indeed. We spent most of the week together working on control and learning how to sort out what feelings were his and how to block out the rest. Granted, most of that time was spent between the sheets, but I don't regret it at all. He was an excellent study, and that's how I found out he was my mate. He wears a starburst mark on the back of his neck and with it, he gains stronger abilities in picking up on emotions and blocking them.

Next, but definitely not least, was my sour Shifter. I was in need of letting off some steam. My men were busy and there weren't any souls in need of another round of torture, so I headed to the fight ring! There, standing in the middle, with sweat and blood splattered over his body and his skin torn open at his knuckles, was a naked Jessup Cloak—he was magnificent and proudly standing there in all his glory. His short black hair was plastered to his scalp and his muscular torso was heaving from the fight he'd just won. His green eyes were laser focused on his opponent until two men came in and dragged him away. Jessup had muscles on top of muscles that rippled in his six-foot frame as he paced back and forth in that ring waiting for the next one to approach.

The rage that rolled off of him called to the black tendrils that coil inside me. I found my perfect outlet for the night, and that man, that magnificent beast, did not disappoint. One night with him turned into multiple, and I just couldn't let him go. Who knew I needed an angry bear to complete me. I knew he was my last mate when his starburst showed up on his left shoulder and I felt complete. Something inside of me just clicked and I felt at peace, balanced like I never knew possible.

Shaking myself out of my memories, I take in my outfit and smile. I'm wearing a cute Ivy summer dress with a plunging neckline and open-back design. I must say, I did an excellent job designing this myself. I especially like how the halter tie makes for easy access. My burgundy hair is done up in soft curls that cascade down my back, framing my bright blue eyes with their long lashes. Carl always says they are my best features. I loved the fact that the color stays even in my demon form. I apply some lip gloss over my rosy lips, slip on my lace-up sandals, and smile. Tomorrow will be my last day of doing my morning routine in this room for a while. Around this time tomorrow, I'll be on Earth taking on a new life with my men, and I can't wait, but first, I need to tie up loose ends.

With my wedding dress in hand, I walk out of my design studio with thoughts of surprising Matthew in his office at the school. He recently moved his stuff over to the Administration building because he wanted to be prepared to take over as soon as we got back from Earth. In twenty years, we will be back and taking over the title of Council Leaders of Nova. I've passed up the leadership for eons now, but after talking with the guys, we've all agreed that we'll step up and take over for the elders that want to retire. I've been putting off my responsibilities long enough. I guess one can only play so long before having to grow up. And since my men have been offered the job with me, we can do anything.

"Lilith!" A wheezing voice calls out, bringing my steps to a halt. Looking over my shoulder, I see a scrawny young man jogging up the sidewalk. I roll my eyes because I know this man, and I don't need the drama. He's one of Adam's assistants, and if he's coming to see me, then Adam must need something last minute before my vacation.

"Yes?" I say with annoyance. Adam is the last person I want to see today. The young man finally reaches me and bows low, showing his reverence. At least Adam taught this one well, though it could be that I flayed the last one alive.

"I'm sorry to disturb you, Mistress. My master, Adam, has asked for your assistance in Hell. He said it was urgent and gave me nothing more," he whispers in fear, keeping his head down.

Ugh. Simpletons, I swear!

The fear rolling off this servant brings a small smile to my face even though I feel the anger rise just underneath my skin.

"Where is he?" I growl out between my teeth.

"Waiting for you in his office, Mistress," he grovels.

Without waiting for him to reply, I swing my wedding dress over my shoulder and conjure up a portal leading right outside his office. I feel my body change back into my demon form as I step into hell. My skin turns a bright burgundy color as my black spider-webbed wings shoot out the back of my dress and lay against my back. My tail swishes back and forth with the irritation of being here instead of back home. In lieu of horns like most demons, I have beautiful white glowing tendrils that line my hairline and fall down my cheeks.

He, at least, got smart over the years and put up a block so I couldn't pop right into his office, but it doesn't stop me from barging right in like I own it. What am I saying? I do own it. All of Hell is mine. Since I was the first of my kind and I was cast out and into this pit, it belonged to me. I became its ruler, but having that title and that responsibility soon got tiring and I appointed my bestie to the job. I wanted to explore and didn't have the drive to lord over people day in and day out like Lucifer did. So he became the figurehead.

Flinging the door open, I walk in and look around. Instead of an office filled with books, there's a big oak desk with a substantial, high-back chair, and plaques and pictures of himself are dotted all over the walls. Some of them even have a few important people over the years cheesing next to him. He still has that obnoxious self-portrait of himself and King Louis the VIII hanging over his fireplace.

His office hasn't changed since the last time I was here. Was that five years ago or ten? I can never keep track of time when it comes to Hell and its operation. Every level has its own time zone, per se. For instance, the highest level has no difference in time, while in the seventh circle of Hell, you spend one day there, and it's the equivalent to a week in Purgatory. Lucky for me, I'm housed on the first level along with the stronger and prominent demons that have the most power. And then you have Adam, the first human that lost his soul to the underbelly of Hell. He has the honorary position here, but that doesn't mean his shit don't stink.

"Lilith! Nice to see you. Please come on in." Adam's deep sultry voice purrs, and all I see is red. And I'm not talking about the walls. This fucker is ruining my afternoon.

"Yes, yes, I know. What the fuck do you want, Adam?" I say, clenching my teeth.

"Oh, don't be like that, Lilith. Here. Look, I even had your favorite drink made to show you how sorry I am to call you away before your departure," Adam says, pushing his blond hair out of his gray eyes. He motions to the drinks laid out on the table in front of him, but I'm in no mood. Yes, it's customary to sit down and have a drink while you talk shop, but I'm hoping to quickly answer his questions and get back home.

"Cut the crap! I don't have time for your nonsense today." I lay my dress on the back of the sofa as I walk over to stand in front of him.

"Tsk. Tsk. Lilith. You know the rules. We drink and then do this talk. I promise this won't take long. I just need help in setting up some stuff before you leave," he assures me and reaches for his Hell's Fireball shot. Since when did he change from Bourbon?

"Fine, but make it quick," I say and reach for my Peek-a-Boo pucker shot, throwing it back in one swoop.

Slamming down my drink, I throw my hands on my hips and let the glass fall to the floor, staining his carpet. *Like I care in keeping his precious rooms clean.* I glare down at Adam. He really is handsome on the outside, but he is pure sludge on the inside, and that's saying something coming from a Demon. I like to do evil things. It's what I do. It's who I am. I take pleasure in sinful activities, but that doesn't mean I'm malicious about it, or skin babies alive. This Demon has standards, but the slick snake that's sitting in front of me, he's almost worse than L.A.M.B. put together. Those boys—Lucifer, Astaroth, Murmur, and Beelzebub—are inseparable, and the biggest assholes you could run into. Yet, they're my best friends; they have been since the beginning, and I don't know what I would do without them. Adam has nothing on them if they put their mind to it, but he has given them a run for their money at times, all on his own.

Adam shifts in his seat and pulls at his light blue sweater. "Relax, Lilith. Have a seat so we can *talk.*" He pats the cushion next to him, and my hackles raise.

"Just get on with it, Adam. I don't have time for this. I was just here yesterday. Why didn't you tell me whatever it is when I was here then?"

The room starts to sway, and I blink my eyes against the blurriness.

What the...

I reach out to grab the arm of the sofa and miss, crashing to the floor face first. *Ouch!*

Adam's voice floats over to me on waves of dizziness. "Well, Lilith. I told you to have a seat."

The last thing I feel is a sharp stabbing ache in my back, causing blinding agony to crash through my body before nothingness descends upon me.

CHAPTER 3
Weakling

Carl

Turning back to my computer, I quickly type in the formula for the correct antidote. I can't wait to show my love that she was right, adding in the extra ingredient did balance out the unstable concoction. Saving the file, I power down the computer, saying my final goodbyes to this side of medicine. I plan to continue my work while we are gone, but focus more on the human aspect of things since we will be on Earth. I'm sure plenty of humans could use the knowledge I bring to the table. I just have to be careful not to share too much, or I could be tipping the lid before we are ready.

Indeed, it will be a lot easier to share our existence with the humans on Earth once we take over on the council, but I have to be careful until then. These next twenty years will be trying, but I'm looking forward to it. I never thought I would ever live this type of life, let alone get married after leaving the Fae kingdom. I was kicked out and shunned almost a thousand years ago. I left behind my royal birthright—by no choice of mine—to pursue my love of science and magic. Or at least that's what I tell myself. The real story is much darker.

As the crown prince of the Spring court, I was obligated to visit other kingdoms and because of this, I ended up becoming the perfect pawn in someone's game. With the murder of the Summer court's crown prince, I found myself disowned, stripped of the only life I knew, and forbidden to ever return. I knew what the reason behind this was, but I chose to look at it for what it really was: freedom. I was given a new life. A chance to choose what I wanted in my life. The blackmail that came from the King of the Elves was a blessing in disguise and gave me a clean slate to leave that horrid lifestyle behind. I left with my head held high and joined the Academy at a much later age than expected.

I was graciously allowed to pursue my study and learned how to control my magic and combine it with my love of science. I'm unique in the fact that my magic doesn't have a class. I'm able to help manipulate elements in salves and healing ointments on the spot with a conduit. The best way to describe it is to give me a patient in pain, and I'm able to heal them by taking the salve and putting it on them. My magic attunes to what they need and works to change the cream to heal them. I guess the simplest way to say that was: I'm a natural healer. I just enjoy the idea of blending magic and science to make a better world, and I'm on the brink of that.

I wouldn't have been able to get this far if it wasn't for the Academy taking in a runaway Fae boy, and the help of a Demon—no, no, she's more than that. She's the original Demon, my love, the glue that keeps us together. She's my everything. My mate!

That alone should be an anomaly, since Demons don't have mates. Most demons just form legions and say they are all mates, but that's not entirely accurate. Since Lilith is one of the most powerful beings there is, she's also the most fragile and susceptible when it comes to her mind, and she needs mates to help keep her balanced. That's where the need for mates comes into play, and she's the only one that needs them. I'm just lucky that I'm one of them. If I could, I would show off my starburst mark that's between my shoulder blades everyday.

I'm practically giddy to head to Earth and start this new chapter in my long life. I feel like that young Fae man walking into class and spotting the hottest Demon in the whole realm all over again. It was the Fates that brought her to me. I was beyond shocked that she talked to me that day, so when she started talking about particle physics, I about died. A beauty that had brains too? Unheard of.

She was a creature I'd never seen before, so when she had first brought Daniel home, I had not taken it lightly at first. There was a part of me that felt like I was lacking, even though it's my nature as Fae to have multiple partners. I wanted to be enough for my love, but I quickly understood that Daniel did bring a lighter aspect to our dynamic. He made her laugh and took her dancing while I stimulated her intellectual side. After that revelation, it was easier to accept Matthew and Jessup when Lilith brought them into the Harem. Matthew was the sensitive Mage that kept up with her emotional needs, and Jessup gave her the Alpha vibes she craved. All of us were needed to fulfill her needs, and we were glad to do it.

Knock. Knock.

Before I could say come in, my door opens up, and there standing in the entry is my goddess herself.

I shoot up in my seat and plaster the biggest smile on my face. I love it when she comes to surprise me. Fates, I love this woman.

"Lilith, Dearest. What brings you by? You know you're supposed to take it easy today. You need to save your strength for the trip to Earth tomorrow," I say, babying her as she enjoys. I walk around my desk to greet her, opening my arms for her to rush into them, but stop short when I notice her look. A frown mars her beautiful face, and I'm lost as to the reason.

"Let me ask you this, Carl," she says, throwing me a hateful look. It throws me for a loop, and I take an involuntary step back, dropping my arms.

"Dearest, what is wrong?" I ask as my stomach plummets.

"Do you think I'm weak?"

"No! Of course not!" My throat suddenly feels dry with where this line of questioning is going.

"Then why would you think I would need to *rest*, huh? I'm not a weak *human* that needs to be taken care of." She places her hands on her hips, and her eyes start glowing red.

"I never s—"

"Or is that what you're hoping to get with a trip to Earth? Are you looking to find one? I know how *fascinated* you are with them." Her anger is palpable, and all I can do is stand there dumbfounded.

"NO!" I manage to get out through my dry throat.

"Look, Carl, I'm going to Earth without you. Don't follow me, and go on and live your life. Move on and have kids."

"What? Where is this coming from, Lilith?" I say, stepping closer to her. I'm just not understanding what is going on. This morning she was so happy. What has changed in the past five hours or so?

"This shouldn't be a surprise. I mean, look at you," Lilith says and points at me, halting me once again in my spot. Looking down, I take in my appearance. My white lab coat is a little rumpled, but other than that, I'm still wearing my glasses, and I know my black wavy hair is a bit disheveled. She had always told me she liked the 'nerdy' look though. Hell, that's one of the reasons I wore the glasses, even though I didn't need them.

"I don't understand." I look back at her and find her snarling at me.

"You are a sniveling, *weak-blooded* Fae that doesn't even have his heritage anymore. Can I even call you Fae when you've given up the name? Why would I want someone like you? What would you truly bring to my life?" Her words are barbs of the thickest Huckabee tree, piercing truly to my soul.

"You don't mean that," I say with conviction.

"You disgust me," she growls.

"Lilith! This isn't right." I shake my head and step closer. This isn't my Lilith. That I know for sure. Something is wrong.

"We're over," she says.

"Please," I beg, dropping to my knees as tears flow down my face as she says the last words to destroy me.

"I release you, Carl Steinbeck, from my love and honor," she says, walking out and slamming the door behind her.

She just left me. She just revoked my life and the binding that I made to her when we pledged ourselves to each other. I don't feel anything magical happen to me besides the emotional pain that seeps into my bones as I sink fully to the floor. I'm grateful at least for the emptiness because breaking the bond, I was told, could quickly kill the Fae who makes it. Maybe Lilith is right, I'm not Fae anymore, so perhaps I'm not even worth dying as one.

CHAPTER 4
Bloody Mary?

Daniel

*I*f *I didn't know better, I would say I was a Pride Demon instead of a Vampire.* Looking around my apartment, I just can't decide what to pack. Yes, most of the stuff I could get on Earth, but I don't want to say goodbye to my babies. Looking over at my cufflinks and shoe collection, my heart breaks a little bit.

I still don't understand why I can't take all of them. While Carl collected diplomas and Jessup got grizzly trophies for his fights, I collected cufflinks and shoes. Though they were surely going to bring theirs to Earth, Lilith has forbidden me from bringing my entire collection. I can only bring thirty pairs! Who in the world can live with only thirty pairs of shoes?

My woman is nuts, certifiably crazy, but I always did have a thing for the loony ones. Who knew that I would have a mate? When that starburst showed up on my right shoulder—after my first night with her—I was ecstatic. Not only did I find the love of my life, but a few of my powers got a boost also. I didn't need to drink blood as often, I was stronger, faster, and my endurance definitely paid off in the bedroom.

My mother said I would once get caught up in my wild ways and reap what I sowed, and boy did I that night at Double D. When I first saw Lilith, I knew right away that I had to have her. Of course, I never expected her to bring me into the pre-existing relationship she had with Carl, but he was a decent man, more brains than brawn if you ask me. But since he made Lilith happy, I wasn't gonna harp on him too much. Besides, he didn't throw a fit when I took Lilith drinking on the weekends and got up to mischief in those booths. Damn, the things she could do.

I often joked she was a dangerous Triple Threat. Tail, Tongue, and Tits! Just thinking about it was making me hard. Adjusting my erection, I look longingly at my spare room before closing the door on my collection —*farewell, sweeties. I will see you again in twenty years.* Who knows, maybe Earth will have decent pairs that I'll bring back with me to add.

I head into the kitchen to grab some blood, wine, and a glass. I'm sure Lilith will allow me between those juicy thighs tonight so I can feed, but it always helps to top off before then. Pouring a decent amount of blood into my cup, I mix in some red wine and stir. I wonder what it will be like for us on Earth. The last time I was there was years ago. Actually, probably longer than that. My parents were still alive, and we were living in Romania. We owned a castle that was situated on a hilltop, overlooking the beautiful countryside. Our servants were sweet, and our subjects loved us.

Then one crazy fucker took our name and said he belonged to the Vlad empire. He started wars, impaling heads on stakes and calling himself a Vampire. Now come on, who's fucking cheesy enough to do that? Yes, we were vampires, but we didn't go around bringing attention to ourselves. I was out securing new land, so I wasn't home when he decided to make the four-day trip and impale my mother and father to our own entrance of the castle. Hell, if you planned on taking our name, at least go all out. He didn't even take our land, but after seeing your parent's heads on pikes set out to greet you, the idea of staying turns sour. That evening, a stranger approached me and said, "It is time to go home, back to Nova." Well shit, I didn't even know the place existed before this person showed up, but I changed my name from Vlad to Abernathy and didn't look back.

I don't know if I even want to visit my old home when we go back. Last I heard, it's not only a tourist trap but a national monument. To make matters worse? They named it after some guy that made a movie about Vampires. Bran Castle. That's not the name of it, yet that's the one sitting on the land if you look on Google maps.

Pulling myself out of my fucked up head, I down my drink in a gulp and set it back down as someone knocks. I walk over and open the door to see Lilith standing there in all her glory. My eyes travel over her body as I take in her sandals and follow them up along her black dress—*huh? Didn't she have an ivy summer dress laid out for today?* I continue my perusal of her figure until I reach her brown eyes—w*ait. What? Brown?* She has blue eyes. Before I can question anything, they're blue again. Damn, it must be the light.

"Don't get too comfortable with what you see," Lilith says, brushing past me. She walks over to stand next to my kitchen island, looks over at my drink, and scrunches her nose up in disgust.

Well, that's new.

"Don't tell me you don't like this brand of wine? I swear we will have better once we get to Earth. I'm thinking the best from Paris, France. I just needed to top off before tonight," I say, picking up the bottle and putting it away.

"It's not the wine, and you know it," she hisses.

"Really? Then what is it now? Because this mood swing doesn't become you at all." I smile, poking fun at her. I know she gets into her serious moods, but I've always been able to make her laugh. This 'bitchy' thing she has going on is definitely not the Lilith I've been with for over 300 years.

"It's the blood. The way you take it. It's disgusting," she says with a sneer on her face.

Her words alone almost knocked me over. Blood? I'm a fucking Vampire. Of course, there is blood.

"How am I supposed to take it, Lilith? Through osmosis?" I ask, my voice turning hard. "I'm a Vampire! I have to drink it to live!"

Her glare is the only response she gives as we stare at each other for a few moments. I've never seen this side of her, though, but now I'm wondering if I've just been blind this entire relationship.

"Oh, I understand that, but you shouldn't be doing it out in the open, Daniel. Keep it as your dirty little secret behind closed doors." She nonchalantly flips her hair, and I see red.

"Dirty. Little. Secret? WHAT THE FUCK, LILITH?" I yell. "This coming from the Demon known to play with the blood from her victims. How many times did we fuck on their corpses and include blood play, and NOW you have a problem?" I pull at the short strands of my hair and roar.

My body is tight as a coil while Lilith stands there motionless as I fall apart in front of her. *How dare she?*

"I'm going to Earth without you, and I suggest you find someone to move on with. Maybe someone who can deal with your...little handicap. Maybe have some little vamp offspring that will give you eternal love. Satan knows you need it," she condescendingly says. "Oh, and I release you, Daniel Abernathy, from my love and honor," she says flippantly and walks out the door.

Picking up the glass in front of me, I throw it across the room. It slams against the door and shatters into a thousand pieces, just like my heart. How can the love of my life reject me?

CHAPTER 5
Little Dick Man

Lilith

I knew better than to trust the drink sitting on that table. That little fucker! And I do mean *little*, no wonder he had issues. God 'blessed' him with the world's smallest dick. No wonder Adam was pissed, made in God's image, huh? Well, in that case, that might explain why God was an asshole. He had little man syndrome.

Looking around the dark room, I try to let my eyes adjust —this room I don't recognize at all. I try to sit up, only to find that I can't. I'm beyond weak, and I feel my wings brush against a wall. Spreading them out further, I can tell I'm in a cage. A. FUCKING. CAGE. Rage boils up through my pores, and instead of seeing black, red now tints my vision and then puckers out.

Damnit! What did Adam hit me with? Obviously, my drink was laced with something that would knock out my powers.

My left-wing rustles involuntarily from being cramped up against a wall, and pain shoots down my spine. Moving my tail up, it grazes something sticking out of the base of my wing. Wrapping it around the handle of a knife, I take in a breath to prepare to rip it out when a thought occurs to me. If he laced the drink, what else is he willing to do?

This might not just be any knife stuck in my back. My tail tentatively starts to gently pull the knife out when blazing heat sears up my spine and freezes my lungs for a few moments. My tail drops down to the floor as I wheeze out shuddering breaths. *Shit! That bitch hurts.*

I have no clue where I am, or what's going to happen next. The worst part, I have no clue what's happening to my mates!

'Your mates are the least of your worries.'

My eyes go wide as I hear a voice in my head that I don't recognize, but understanding quickly slams into me. I've been alive since the beginning of time, so I've seen it all. I used to sit around the campfire and listen to the other Demons talk about their first time breaking Hell's barrier and possessing humans.

'How?' I growl out.

That's the only question I have for the Demons that somehow possessed me. There has to be more than one inside of me. It makes no sense that only one low-level Demon could overthrow me even with a weapon stabbed into my back, no matter what Adam had put on it.

It's confirmed when I hear multiple voices laugh in my mind.

'Aww, poor Lilith, can't figure shit out.' A squeaky voice chuckles.

'She wants to know how we got here. Should we tell her?' a guttural voice answers.

'Nah. That's too easy. Sleep, Lilith,' a voice demands, and I'm plunged into darkness once again.

CHAPTER 6
Emotionally Drained

Matthew

Sitting back in my desk chair, I look over my new office while sipping at my tea. I needed a small break before tackling the last few boxes and meeting up with the guys. I don't want anything to pull me away from my first time going to Earth with Lilith. I know how crazy that seems with me being over 400 years old, but if it wasn't one thing, it was another.

I've been to Earth before, actually, I was born there, but my time there didn't end on a high note. My parents were magic users, and they kept to themselves mostly. My father worked as a farmer, growing and cultivating the land. It was the safest line of work, and it allowed him to use his magic to grow the crops during times of harvest. My mother was a midwife. She loved healing the women without them knowing and bringing healthy babies into the world. That was actually how I met my first friend, Dorcus Good.

My mother helped deliver her and her younger sister. I didn't think much of what my family did until the witch hunters came for them. Dorcus was thrown in jail at the age of four with her mother, and my family was taken along with them.

My magic started to manifest early, around my sixth birthday, so my grandparents were called upon, and I stayed home that day instead of following my family to work. I would have gone down with the hundreds of names accused as witches during the Salem Witch Trials. It still makes me sick to my stomach to this day thinking about how I would have swung from those ropes if it wasn't for the Fates and how they intervened.

It's taken years to understand I wasn't to blame and to let go of the guilt, but try telling my grandparents to do the same and you'll get a big negative. They have been the reason why I haven't gone back to Earth since then. When I've had the chance, I've either had to cancel trips to take care of them, or their guilt ate at my resolve until I gave in. This time though, nothing is stopping me from being with Lilith and the rest of my family. I'm ready to start a life. We've even talked about adoption while we're there since Lilith can't have children, but that's if what Carl is working on doesn't work. It's everything I was hoping for.

A knock on my door pulls me out of my musings. "Come in." Setting down my cup of tea, I straighten my jacket before bringing my attention to the door. Standing at the entrance is my old classmate and dearest friend, Abi. Her petite frame is dressed in a yellow sundress today, and her plum hair is down to her shoulders.

"Did you hear?" Abi says, waving the paper in front of her face.

"Hear what?" I ask, shaking my head in confusion.

"They found her! The missing Fate," she says, walking in and throwing down the newspaper on my desk. Quirking an eyebrow at her, I pick up the paper and scan the front page.

Missing Fate's Body Found In Stream

Well, fuck! For the past month, Purgatory has been up in arms looking for the missing Fate, Liliwen, and now it looks like they found her. That means they will start looking for a new one, and I guarantee that will take time. There's not much that we know about the Fates, only that there are always three, and once one has passed, one will appear to take their place. I've never heard of a Fate going missing, or even them looking for a new one, but I guess it happens.

"Does it mention what happened to her?" I ask, my stomach churning at the thought of her passing. I take one look at her paling face and decide I don't want to know. "Nevermind. I don't want to know," I say, waving her reply away. The distressed emotion coming off of her is enough to know it's bad.

How does a Fate even die? They are like gods to us, all-powerful and all-knowing. They're the top dogs, followed by the council, which I will be stepping up to when we come back. The so-called 'Leaders of Nova' are really just the governing body with enough power to keep all of us in line, but the Fates hold the real power.

Hell, without the Fates, no one will be able to travel to Earth. They set up the schools around Purgatory to teach us to learn and control our powers. Once we learned those, we went to the Gauntlet. Think of it as the final exam to end all exams. I barely survived that nightmare of a task. The Gauntlet is a week of hell that makes you encounter monsters and situations to test how you handle yourself. Each day you lined up and prayed to the Fates sent you somewhere decent. I had to survive in a swamp and fend off the monsters that lived there, but at least I had a group of students with me. Abi saved my life more than once during that week. She always said I returned the favor when I helped set her up with her mate. Either way, our friendship has blossomed to what it is today.

"Do you know what this means?" Abi says, bouncing on her feet.

"Yeah, it means I'm leaving at the right time," I say, getting out of my chair. I grab one of my boxes and move it over to the empty bookshelf.

"No! Silly. It means someone will gain the late Fates power and transform into the next Fate. I heard that anyone could, even a Vampire!" Abi squeals. I can't help but laugh at her excitement. I move back over to Abi and look down at her five-foot-four frame. She's always been comfortable as a Vampire, but she's been curious about the unknown for as long as I can remember, and the Fates are the pentacle of that.

"If anyone deserves to earn those powers, Abi, it would be you." I smile down at her and pull her in for a friendly hug. Ever since school, she's been like a little sister to me, and I want what's best for her.

A throat clearing makes me pull away and look up to see my Queen standing in the doorway with a frown on her face. Immediately I'm put on guard. Shit, maybe she heard some bad news.

"Hi, Lilith! Are you excited about heading to Earth in the morning?" Abi greets Lilith with a smile.

I watch as Lilith curls her lip and looks Abi up and down like she smells something foul. "I don't know if that's any of your concern, but yes, I am. Now, do you mind giving us a moment to talk?" she says, stepping into the office and giving Abi the evil eye. Abi gives me a tentative smile as she wishes us a safe journey, waves goodbye, and slips out of the room.

Focusing back on Lilith, I catch a few emotions surfacing but I push those to the back of my mind when I see a small smirk on her lips.

"Was that really necessary, Lilith? You didn't have to be

rude about needing a moment with me. You know she's just a friend," I explain in confusion.

I take a moment to assess her emotions, and anger is rolling off of her—with a hint of glee. That's unlike her. She loves Abi, and for the life of me, I don't understand what's going on.

"I guess not, but it doesn't hurt to remind her that you're above her station," she says coyly. Annoyance pricks my skin as she slams Abi's lower station. She isn't a strong vampire, but what she lacks in strength, she makes up with knowledge and charisma. I watch as Lilith sways her hips as she walks over to my desk. Leaning against it, she picks up one of the trinkets and gives it a curious look before wrinkling her nose in disgust and puts it down.

"So, what did you want to talk about that made you so rudely dismiss Abi like that?" My annoyance is clear in my voice.

"Well, it's a good thing I did, else you might have caught yourself in an even more compromising position," she accuses, yet it's not jealousy I'm picking up.

"Oh yeah? Then why does that excite you? You're acting like it bothers you, yet you're happy about something," I accuse.

Her body language and emotions are at odds with each other. The only time she does this is during foreplay, trying to play all coy and shit, but even that is easy for me to pick up. This is something completely different.

"Let me guess, you're trying to read my emotions again," she sneers.

"You're blasting me with it, but yes. You know this, though. I can't count how many times you've told me it's one of my best qualities. I'm able to read you like a book," I say, walking over to her. I rub my hands up her arms and smile as goosebumps erupt along her skin, that is until revulsion hits me, and I drop my hands. "I disgust you?" I choke out.

She moves away from me and starts to rub her arms from where I touched her. A knife stabs into my heart, watching her wipe my touch away, as if it's something vile.

"You have no boundaries, Matthew. You're constantly invading my privacy, and I just don't feel comfortable with you anymore," she whines and moves closer to the door.

"What? No, Lilith. That's not what I'm doing at all," I reassure her and take a step closer to her, where panic hits me straight to my chest. Her fear of me almost sinks me to my knees as I reach out to stabilize myself against my desk. What the hell is going on? Since when is she terrified of me?

"You might not think that's what you're doing, but you are, and I can't handle it anymore. You've been so wrapped up in reading emotions that you can't stand on your own two feet without leaning on them. That doesn't make you strong, Matthew, that makes you *weak*," she snaps.

"You don't mean that," I whisper.

"What do my emotions tell you?" She raises her chin. "I'm going to Earth without you, and I suggest you move on. Go have those disgusting brats you wanted to fill your house with. You might as well since I was never going to go through with it or take the oath with you. I would have just resented you later in life for it." Her emotions are all over the place, but the underlying one was joy. She's happy that she's ripping my heart out and serving it up on a bloody platter.

My Queen, the love of my life, is tearing me apart one shredded piece at a time. A black hole opens up, and I feel myself fall into despair as she just gives me a tight smile and waves. She walks out of the door, and my life, as if my soul isn't shattering into a million pieces and may never be whole again.

CHAPTER 7
Rabid Beast

Jessup

Cracking my neck, I take in my opponent standing across from me. It was Talon's last day visiting Nova, and I promised him a match before he went back to his own pack. He's a good guy that at times I envy, but not for his good looks or his massive size, which overshadow my six-foot frame. No, what I envy is how he isn't controlled by his rage like I am. Though, if you look at that alone, it means I'm stronger than him, but at times I wish it wasn't the case.

The more rage a Shifter has, the more power they are said to possess, and the forms we have represent that. Most Shifters have two, a large and small form. Talon's smaller form is a tan and black falcon with golden eyes. His larger form is a polar bear that's right at home on the other side of the mountain, far North from here. His long golden hair is pulled back into a bun at the base of his skull, and his bare chest is covered in tattoos. Flecks of gold shine out between his light brown eyes, signaling his power is close to the surface.

"I'm gonna eat you alive; you know that, right?" His deep timber booms out, bringing a hush to the crowd.

I smile back and crack my knuckles as I watch him shift his stance. Once you've crossed over the threshold of the sacred circle, all friendships are put to the side. It's a time to allow your inner beast out to play. Shifter against Shifter, beast against beast. It isn't always an equal match-up, but if you have a grudge against someone, this is how you take it out, in the fights.

This match, though, we need to feel the blood flow in our natural forms. Fists, legs, and teeth. Nothing is off the table, and if you can partially shift, then all the better. It takes extreme concentration to partially shift or a lot of rage to fuel you, and I can do both. Not sure if Talon can, but we're about to find out.

Talon circles to the left, and I follow him with my eyes as we assess each other. It's common knowledge everyone has two forms since we formed packs, but I have a secret weapon. I have more than two, and I pull my wolverine to the surface just as Talon lunges for me with the swiftness of his falcon. He tackles me to the ground, and I quickly shift my hips, throwing us off course. Rolling us forward head over our shoulders, I spread out my legs, stopping our momentum, and we roll to a stop as I land on top of him. I throw a right hook before his face even comes into focus, and I hear a crunch as my fist connects. I'm so focused on keeping my balance from the force of my punch that I don't see the jab coming in for my ribs until it is too late.

I grunt in pain as air wheezes out of my lungs. The brutal force of the hit causes me to roll and fall off of Talon. Quickly pulling myself up to a standing position, I watch as Talon pops his jaw back into place. Rolling my shoulders and pushing down the pain in my side, I observe Talon as his eyes watch me like a...well, hawk.

He lunges again, but this time I'm ready for him. I feint right and flank him, bringing up my knee to hit him in the diaphragm, causing air to swoosh out. But before I can move my leg, he latches on with his black claws and digs in, immobilizing me in a pretty awkward stance. Before I can try to flip myself out of his hold, he throws me into the air, spiraling towards the other side of the circle. Landing with a grunt, I see spots start to cloud my vision before the darkness of the rage overtakes me.

"Jessup! STOP!"

"He's going to kill him."

Voices filter in slowly, and my vision slowly clears to the point that all I see is blood. Hands pull me away and help support my body as I come to and focus in on Talon's motionless body at my feet.

Shit!

I take a step forward to check on Talon, but another Shifter I don't recognize is already checking his pulse. "He's still alive," he announces and stands. Grabbing my bloody hand, he thrusts it up in the air yelling, "Jessup's the winner!"

The crowd erupts in chants of victory. Everyone gathers around me and hoists me up onto their shoulders as a couple of Shifters drag Talon's body off to the medical center. The crowd surges and the atmosphere is charged from the bloodshed. Shifters prey on violence and chaos, so I can't help but ride the high of the win and laugh as they celebrate with me. I know there will be a part of me that will miss these fights, but Daniel has already agreed to spar with me to help me with the need for violence. It won't be as potent, but I'm willing to try this new chapter with my family for the next couple of decades. I happen to look over and see Lilith standing off in the tree line. Her long hair is pulled up into a loose bun and she wears a long, dark halter dress. *That doesn't look like the dress she had laid out from last night.*

"Let me down," I bellow, and I'm dropped to the ground. Not wasting a second, I push through the crowd until a path opens. Rushing to Lilith, I pick her up and spin her around in one swoop. Slowing to a stop, I slam my mouth down on hers only to feel her jerk away in response.

Pulling back, I look down to see her ire focused on me.

"What the FUCK, Jessup?" she hisses, pushing out of my arms. She pulls part of her dress away from her body and scowls up at me. "Look at this! It's ruined," she cries out. She angrily wipes the blood from where I had kissed her, shakes her head, and moves deeper into the woods with me following her.

"Lilith. What's the matter? You should be celebrating with me! I defeated Talon, *and* I didn't kill him," I say, stepping in front of her. "Come on. What's wrong?"

My energy is through the roof, and I find myself bouncing on the balls of my feet as I wait for her answer. I'm like a little toddler hyped up on too much candy.

"What's wrong?" Lilith asks, looking at me in disbelief. "Look at you! Your rage is getting out of hand. You *almost* killed a man. I can't be with someone who can't control themselves," she sneers at me in disgust. Her blue eyes flash with anger as she inhales sharply. She takes a step back from me, and it's like a douse of ice water that gets thrown on me. "I thought you were better than that. What kind of *powerful* Shifter are you if all you do is leave destruction in your wake?"

That fury that is a constant ember in my soul flares up into a raging inferno. I know my blue eyes are glowing from the rolling violence I'm scarcely restraining. The burning in my gums is the first sign of my bear trying to break free and reach for who he considers his mate. Although, he's not reaching because he wants to get closer to the mate bond, something's wrong. He's not feeling it right now and he's pissed. *What is happening?* The sensation shocks me enough to hold back the change of my bear.

"My parents are just as powerful, and they've never killed anyone. What makes you think I would?" I growl.

"Your parents are now hermits, living in a hut somewhere in the mountains. Of course, they won't hurt anyone. They are all alone, Jessup," she shrieks, throwing her arms in the air. "I can't live in isolation, and I refuse to," she says, pointing to herself.

Those words cut deeper than any claw or pair of teeth that I've taken in the fights. I would rather take any physical pain than what my mate is telling me. Doesn't she realize what she's doing to me? Denying me, her mate, is physically causing me pain. Grabbing my chest, I fall to my knees with tears brimming in my eyes.

"We don't have to live that way. I would never harm you or the other guys. Please, Lilith," I plead, the act is unbecoming of me. I don't even know what I'm begging for, but I don't like where this is leading. She looks at me with cold, dead eyes and my heart plummets. The love that once filled her to the brim has run its course.

"The only way you'll be able to survive is to be isolated. So, I suggest you go and find someone to give you pups and move on. Your bloodline is the only good thing about you," she says, turning and weaving through the woods.

The agonizing pain is too much to hold back, and I feel my Timberwolf break through and take over. I give myself over to the pain. The last memory I have is hearing the lonely howl of a broken wolf.

CHAPTER 8
Lilith had a little L.A.M.B

Lilith

Grinding metal stirs me back to consciousness, arousing my wings. My appendages bristle and pain shoots up my spine, making me gasp.

"Lilith?" A deep, dark, and sinister voice calls out. That voice is known to cause delicious shivers to race down a lover's spine in the heat of passion. Though, it could easily be a cause for panic because that also means he's coming for his pound of flesh. In my case, all I feel is relief, because Bez has found me.

"In here," I croak out a whisper. I have no idea how long I've been stuck in this black void, but it's long enough that my body hurts and I'm extremely dehydrated. The possessing Demons within me have done nothing but cackle with glee as they have practiced trying to take control of my body. I've come to find out they quickly drain me when I fight against them, but that could be caused by the fucking dagger stuck in my back blocking my powers.

Light penetrates the darkness and I only get a few moments to look around the bare cell before a massive body blocks off the light to the room. Unable to make out who just walked in, a slight tingle of fear penetrates me for a brief moment. Maybe this isn't Beelzebub after all. Suddenly, the figure conjures up fire in his palm and I almost weep with relief as to who it is.

My savior comes in the form of one nasty, mocha-skinned Vengeance Demon, the first to be exact.

"Bez!" I whimper.

He throws his fire into the air, and it hovers, lighting the room. Standing at seven-feet tall, broad shoulders, and a machete hanging off his back, Bez is a sight for sore eyes. His massive black wings flare out behind him and it causes shadows to dance across the floor. I've always been envious of his wings. I love his black feathers whereas my wings are more like spider webs. Beelzebub kneels as flames dance in his chocolate orbs when he takes in my appearance.

"Thank Satan, you're okay. How bad are you hurt?" He grunts out. His eyes flare and he clenches his fist when he sees the knife in my back.

"I'm po—" I choke as my throat closes up and my lungs burn for a moment. Laughter rings out in my head and a voice speaks up.

'You're spelled, Lilith,' the more serious Demon announces.

'You can't say anything about the possession,' the gruttal Demon purrs.

'So good luck getting help!' the squeaky Demon teases.

Fuck! That does complicate things, but there's nothing I can do about it now. One thing at a time. Get out of here, get my revenge, and find my mates. I'm the original Demon, I can take care of the lesser Demons later.

"I'm alive," I squeak out.

He nods and stands back up, taking in the bars on the cage. Heat flares from his palms as he runs his hands over the bars, melting them with Hell Fire. Beelzebub is one of the original angels that fell with me that glorious day long ago, and he has remarkable powers. One of his primary weapons is controlling Hell Fire, but he prefers to use knives to play with. Says it allows him to get 'personal' with his victims, and this is why we are friends. A man after my own heart.

Once the bars vaporize to nothing, I try to move but let out a hiss when my shoulder flares with pain. Damn, I almost forgot about the knife.

Bez reaches in to pick me up, trying his best not to jostle me as I bite my tongue, holding in my moans.

"Sorry," Bez apologizes, and I press my head into his bare, tattooed chest and look up, seeing his brown eyes warm as he adjusts me against him.

"You shaved your head?" I ask, looking up at his head and seeing his thick black antelope horns not obscured by his normally thick curls. He lets out a gruff laugh.

"You've been stabbed in the back, left in the seventh level of Hell, and you're talking about my hair?"

"Yeah, I guess I am." I try to chuckle and end up coughing. Moaning from the pain, I tuck my head back into his shoulder once again.

"Leave it to you to be the one to ask silly questions when it looks like someone wanted you out of the way." A smooth and silky voice purrs to my right. Startled, I look over and see that all of L.A.M.B. has come to my rescue, and I spot Lucifer giving me a curious look. His black suit contrasts against his white, feathered wings that drape over his massive shoulders, forming to his narrow waist. He's looking dapper with his dirty blond hair styled around two tiny onyx horns in soft spikes and his perpetual 5 o'clock shadow lining his angular jaw. His blue-green eyes sparkle as he makes fun of me.

"Thanks, Lucy, but can we get this knife out of my back, please?"

"Your wish is my command," he says, teleporting us with a snap of his fingers.

I recognize Lucifer's room instantly as Bez gently lays me face down on the black leather sofa. We're in his sitting room where he often entertains guests. The black and gray marble interior doubles as a peek into Lucy's personality, plus it's easier to clean the gore off when he becomes unstable.

"Damn, chick-a-dee, who did you piss off?" Murmur asks with his British accent. The original Mischief Demon smirks as he crouches down, pushing his brown hair out of his face. His green eyes sparkle with mirth against his blue skin as he takes in my scowl. There's no horns adorning this demon, oh no, he's too good for that. He does have the longest tail in hell, though, which he often says is representative of his dick size, and his wings are a leathery black and blue like a bat's. His signature black leather jacket reforms over his wings when he takes it on and off. Magic works wonders at times. He's wearing a white henley shirt that forms to his chest. This little fucker is enjoying the idea I got myself into this mess. Everything about him just screams cocky asshole.

"Adam," I growl out, then suck in a breath when Astaroth lightly tries to move the knife.

"Adam, as in your ex-Adam?" Astaroth asks as he pokes at the skin around the knife.

"Yes," I say, hissing. "Will you stop poking at the damn thing and get it out?" I squeak when he hits an awfully sore area.

"It's not that simple, Luv. It looks like that little prick got ya good with a God-blessed dagger of sorts," Murmur says, wiggling his eyebrows.

Scoffing, I turn my head so I'm facing the back of the sofa. Of course that fucker used a dagger that would naturally weaken me, but the question is, what else did he use that allowed me to become possessed? "You're just gonna have to rip it out then. I'll heal, I always do."

"The way your skin is puckering, makes me believe there are barbs digging in. It's gonna be painful. I don't think I'm going to be able to mask it," Astaroth explains.

Well, shit.

He would know since he is versed in all weapons. Hell, he makes most of the weapons in the legions armory.

"It looks to be Iridium and, yes, it is blessed. Whoever made this, did a decent job in disabling your powers to heal. But I doubt they expected me to be here," Astaroth confirms.

"You sure?" Lucifer asks as he moves my hair out of my eyes. Silver depths gaze into my blue eyes, searching for any hesitation.

Taking in a deep breath and feeling a twinge in my shoulder, I let it slowly out and look up at Lucifer. "Yeah," I sigh and nod. I go to take in a deep breath to brace myself, when agony slices through me as the knife slowly tears the ligaments and muscles within me. Black spots cloud my vision while I struggle to take in a breath, only to scream seconds later as I feel the tissue around my wings snap and tear. Muscle spasms rack my body as tears fill my eyes when fire courses along my over-sensitive nerves. Even the Demons inside of me scream in pain. I struggle but can't catch my breath, so with my frozen lungs, I black out.

I awaken to a different type of pain. This one is deep in my soul. Something is very wrong with my men. My connection to them is off. It's a worrisome ache that I've never felt before. Like an old wound that's scabbed over, still fresh enough to cause a constant ache. It will heal differently yet scar the skin.

Sitting up, I rub at the ache in my chest. "How long was I out?" I squeak out to no one in particular. I look around the room and see different expressions of anger and worry dotted on the guys faces. It's Bez, the Vengeance Demon, that speaks.

"You've been out for a couple of days," he says, popping his knuckles. The look of pure malice and eagerness is warring on his face, indicating he's itching for a fight.

Murmur hands me a cold glass of water, and I eagerly drink it down and hand it back, asking for another one. He quickly hands me another glass, and this time I slowly sip it before placing it down on the coffee table. Lucifer gets up and sits down next to me, grabbing my hand. "What happened, Lilith? We thought you were on Earth." I go to answer him when his next words silence me in shock. "It wasn't until we heard rumors that your men were there alone that we figured something wasn't right."

I rub against the ache in my chest as tears gather in my eyes. *Is that what I'm feeling? My men being that far away?* I quickly recall that morning to my friends, explaining how I was getting my wedding dress when Adam's lackey said I was needed. "He somehow spiked my damn drink and stabbed me in the fucking back!" I growl out, my tail whipping in agitation.

"We don't know what all the dagger had on it, but there was a residual spell left on it that we can't distinguish. Are you sure that you're okay?" asked Murmur, his agitation making his British accent strong.

Ignoring his question about my well being, I continue. "You said I was in the seventh level." All the guys nod. "How long was I down there?" I swallow around the lump stuck in my throat as my stomach turns to lead.

"At that level, you were there for three months," Murmur says, and for once there's no humor in his words.

A sob breaks free from my lips as I do the calculations in my head. *Oh Satan. No wonder the ache feels so old and is on its way to healing.*

'*You might as well forget about them now. The damage is already done,*' the serious Demon purrs in my head, but I try to block them out.

"It's been thirteen years?" I choke out and tears fall unbidden as I curl up into myself. The throb in my soul intensifies as if it knows I'm mourning the time I've lost with my loves. I give myself a few minutes to lose it while my mind wonders over what I did know. I've been stuck in the seventh level of hell and no one came to find me. *Adam took me out, but why? What did he have to gain? Why didn't my loves, my* mates, *come find me? Are they okay? What kept them from searching for me?* I'm about to ask if they were okay when I remember what Lucifer had said originally.

I wipe away the remaining tears and look at Lucifer. "What rumors did you hear?"

Lucifer reaches up and adjusts his tie, which is one of his tells that he was nervous. I'm either going to be upset or pissed. My guess is on the latter.

"Ahem. Well, a few months ago, we heard a rumor that your men were starting families of their own," he says and promptly clenches his jaw. Out of my peripheral vision I see the rest of the guys shift, but I can't focus on them.

I close my eyes trying to wade through all the emotions I have coursing through my veins. I'm devastated. This kind of betrayal is unheard of in the supernatural world. Yes, humans leave their loved ones all the time, but mates don't. And for them to actively start a family while I was missing...I'd rather have the knife shoved back into my back. It wouldn't hurt this much. I'm not the type to sit and wallow. Give me a few minutes to grieve and then I'm up to finding answers, and if needed, seek my revenge.

Opening my eyes, I take everyone in. Lucifer is polishing his pocket watch but eyeing me from the corner of his eyes. Bez is sitting on a foot stool, sharpening his machete, holding the whetstone so hard that his knuckles are white. Murmur is wiping down the water glass I just used. Astaroth is just sitting in the chair across from me, staring at the floor with a scowl on his face.

"S-so you're saying you only heard rumors? You don't know that for sure?" I address Lucifer.

"They were from reliable sources," he replies, not making eye contact.

"So what are you going to do next?" Murmur asks as he takes a seat on the other side of me.

"Well, it looks like I need to start at the end." I give Murmur a wicked smile.

"Where's Adam now? Does anyone know?" Astaroth growls out. The first Wrath Demon stands up and starts pacing the room, his red wings pulled tight against his back. Small booming sounds echo around the room as his tail cracks like a bullwhip, and his steps are soundless on the marble floor yet he strides with purpose back and forth in front of the fireplace. Not like we needed the heat, this is hell after all, but it is a nice decoration. His long brown hair floats around his shoulders and ram horns as his anger and power rises with every step.

"Astaroth," I whine and his head swings my way.

"Sorry," he mumbles, reigning in his power, but his blue eyes still have flames burning in the orbs. "I think we need to go hunting," he says and a cruel smile graces his bearded jaw.

CHAPTER 9
This little piggy

Lilith

Finding Adam isn't hard. The little shit is throwing a party in his rooms. I don't know what kind of party, nor do I plan to ask, but I am completely civil in his extraction. I simply knock on the door and when his servant—the one from before—answers, I give him my award winning smile and he pales before Murmur knocks him out. Waltzing in with my best friends following in my wake, I watch as everyone either stares like they are starstruck or shakes with fear as we pass. Talk about a confidence boost. I'm the Queen of Hell, and I should be treated as such. They move in waves to open up a path to the man paling at the sight of me. He starts scrambling around people trying to get away, and a few demons I recognize block his way once it becomes clear who I'm hunting.

They will be rewarded for their efforts later, but right now my only focus is my ex-husband. Pulling Adam out of the room, kicking and screaming, is just the icing on the cake.

Demons and Fallen Angels start to whisper and speculate as to the reason we're dragging Adam away. Let those rumors run rampant, it only causes my infamy to skyrocket. I'd rather have my subjects fear me than see me as weak, and it helps knowing L.A.M.B has my back. Now, to secure my men and my life will be complete once again. But first, I need to find out what happened to them.

The screams flowing out of Adam are music to my ears. I once thought it was a curse that I couldn't escape the man I was given to. The Bible had it all wrong. It wasn't Adam and Eve, that sniveling banshee. Yeah, you read that right. She's a damn banshee, always crying about something. I don't even know if she's still alive. As far as I know, they broke up and Adam has been sticking his wick into anything with a heartbeat. But obviously Adam finally got tired of her crying about everything. Yes, death happens, but apparently not for dear old Adam. God has a sick sense of humor when he paired us up. The first human and the first Demon. Granted, he never thought it would change Adam's soul into an eternal one when I took his innocence.

Even with him being my first, I knew he sucked in bed, just lying there weeping at the beauty of it all. Really? He deserved Eve. When I left, I gave God the finger and convinced a few angels to follow me to the depths of Hell and the bliss it could provide. God decided to create Eve to keep Adam in line and give him a wet hole to occupy his time. Obviously, she wasn't me and she didn't have a backbone, so they deserved each other. Spewing her lies about me is what got Lucifer, my bestie's, attention. It's never a good thing to paint a target on your back when it comes to the ultimate trickster. Her fall from God's grace, as of today, is still his ultimate trophy. That's probably the only part the Bible got right, him tricking her, but I understand why they glossed over that debacle. It's a fucked up story, and it doesn't even have me in it! Who leaves out the main character? Definitely not the book for me, but for those that love it, good for you!

"Lil...Lilith," Adam sputters out as blood and drool dribble down his chin. The pleading in his eyes brings a smile to my cruel lips. He's strapped down on my torture table with the same metal he used to stab me in the back.

"Aww, does little ole Adam finally want to tell me what I want to hear?" I question him, picking up a knife and twirling it.

Bez chuckles in the dark corner. The Vengeance Demon couldn't pass up the chance to join in the fun. We've spent the past two hours carving up my ex. Any other time I might have found his stubbornness admirable, but I'm impatient. I want to know why I was stabbed in the back, thrown into the seventh level of Hell, and what he did to my men because I KNOW he did something.

Walking over to Adam with my next move planned out, I trail the sharp dagger up his arm and across his collar bone, where the small, thin line starts trickling blood. The door opens up and Murmur waltzes in right as I run my knife down Adam's chest.

"Has he squealed yet?" Murmur's jovial voice rings out as he moves some of my instruments on the table and hops on it, swinging his legs.

"He will," I reassure him as I reach for the tube of sulfur

dust that's laying on the table. Pouring a few drops onto the blade, I watch as the steel turns a light yellow as it sets. A coy smile plays at my lips as I trace around the tip of the knife around his areola. Adam pants and whimpers as I slowly make the pass. When he looks up at me, I quickly flick my wrist, slicing his nipple clean off and digging the tip of the knife deep into his pec. He screams until his throat is raw, and I twist the dagger until he blacks out.

"Hmm. The dust was a nice touch," Murmur teases as he gives me a smirk.

That little fucker. Murmur's only saying that because I've finally taken him up on his advice and started using his dust.

"Let me wake him up. It's my turn after all," Bez retorts, pushing off the wall and sauntering over to Adam's feet. I nod and step back far enough to get a good view.

I have a slight bout of my vision going black and I hear chuckling in my head as the Demons voice their opinion.

'Do you think we should make her black out so she can't watch the fun?' the squeaky voice laughs.

'Nah. That would bring too much attention to us, and we don't want that right now. We have to play it cool. We can fuck with her when she's alone though,' the guttural voice replies.

I let out a growl at the blatant audacity of fucking with me. ME, the Queen of Hell! Who were these Demons, and what were their purposes in possessing me? When I asked earlier, they just laughed and refused to answer.

Murmur and Bez arch a brow at my growl but don't comment. *Smart men.* Bez extends his hands and flames lick around his fingers as he trails them closer to Adam's feet. I'm fascinated by how the skin at the bottom of his feet peels and curls up, turning black. The smell is atrocious, but the screams he lets out while jolting awake is a beautiful scene to witness.

Murmur leans over and gives Adam a malicious smile and taunts him, "I see you wanted my attention, little one. Let's see what crazy things are inside that head of yours, shall we?" He places his hands on both sides of Adam's temples, causing my ex to flinch. Murmur closes his eyes and the room starts to darken as he wreaks havoc on Adam's subconscious, trying to focus his mind and will him into telling me what I want to know. After a few moments, Murmur opens his green eyes and seeks out my blue ones before he nods at me. I approach Adam so he will be able to hear my words clearly.

"What did you do to my mates?" My voice is deadly calm as it rings out around the room. Adam's body starts thrashing on the table, almost breaking his restraints. Bez quickly reinforces them with hell fire, melting and remodeling the cuffs solidly back on his arms. Once they are sealed, he leans back against the wall. Adam's body bucks against Murmur's ministrations until suddenly Adam lets out a mournful cry and his body goes limp, resting on the table. I quirk an eyebrow about to ask Murmur what the fuck when Adam starts talking.

"I told them to move on and get a new life without you," he grinds out through clenched teeth.

"That's impossible. They wouldn't leave because *you,* of all people, told them to move on. So what really happened?" I asked, letting out a laugh at his complete bullshit lie.

"They would if they thought it was you." He lets out a wheezing laugh that sends dark blood bubbling out of the corner of his mouth. "Th-those mates of yours were so easily d-duped. It was ef-ef-effortless to break their hearts," he stutters out. Taking in a deep, wheezing breath, he continues, "They left P-purgatory the next day like their asses were on fire," Adam groans. Without conscious thought, I yank out the dagger that's in his right pec muscle and stab him in the nuts. He screams bloody murder and promptly passes out again.

I turn around in frustration and start pacing the room. "You know, this would go a lot faster if you didn't keep making him pass out," Murmur drawls. Standing up, he shakes his hands out and reaches for a water bottle out of the little fridge in the wall. Throwing one to Bez in the corner, he then walks over to the small loveseat situated in the opposite corner of the room. There isn't much in here, but it is stocked with essentials to make sure I don't have to leave a torture session in my 'dungeon' once I've began. A place to sit; water and snacks in the small fridge camouflaged into the wall, a bathroom with a shower hidden behind another wall; and a few changes of clothes. If I really needed to stay down here with some of the more stubborn victims, there was a decent-sized bed behind the shower in the bathroom, but I rarely have to use it.

Bez makes quick work with his water, downing it in a few swallows. Crunching the bottle up in a ball, he begins melting the plastic quickly and reforming it into a clear push dagger. He steps over to Adam's secured hand and splays out his fingers and then promptly starts playing 'Five Finger Fillet.' You know, the game where you stab between the fingers and get faster with each pass. He starts singing. "One, two, three, come play with me. Four, five, six, I'll cut you to bits. Seven, eight, nine, it's killing time. Ten, let's stab you again," he carols and sinks the hardened plastic into Adam's flesh between his thumb and forefinger.

Reawakening, Adam screams, and I quickly get back in his face. Baring my fangs, I snarl, wrapping my long manicured nails around his throat and dig into his flesh.

"Where. Are. My. MATES!" Screaming into his face, I make sure to punctuate every word. Shaking from all the anger flowing in my veins, I start squeezing, like he's my very own stress ball until steady hands pry my bloody finger tips off of Adam's neck.

"Easy there, Lil. You'll rip out his throat and then we'll be up Hell's creek waiting for it to grow back. You want your answers, don't ya?" I stop resisting and Murmur takes that as his answer. "Okay then. Why don't you go back to Nova, clean up, and go for a walk to cool off? Let us work on getting you your answers, okay?" Murmur coos at me like I'm a damn baby. Sighing, I realize he does have a point. I'll end up hurting Adam so bad, we will have to wait for him to regenerate before trying again. Nodding my head, I agree. I'll go and at least clean up since I'm covered in Adam's blood, and that'll maybe clear my head.

CHAPTER 10

An old Friend

Lilith

My shower might have left my skin feeling all tingling and refreshing, but I was still full of turmoil. All during my shower, I battled the Demons in my body trying to stay in control as they made me black out throughout the different points of getting dressed as if they were trying to learn how to work my body. Frustrated about the entire process and the fact I even have them in me, I figure a walk is needed. Dressed in a pair of dark-wash jeans with a crop top hoodie and knee-high boots, I take off for a walk, not having a destination in mind. Besides, I haven't breathed anything besides Hell-tainted air in months—or technically years, but that's not the point.

Two hours later, I find myself strolling within the Ever Woods. Nova's park wasn't doing it for me, too many people. I did stop by the guy's old stomping grounds. Even though we were a solid group, we each had our own homes. It looked completely the same, no dust or rodent signs since the Brownies were paid ahead of time to take care of our houses while we were away. Most of the things were untouched, but a few items were missing. Like Daniel's favorite pair of black leather suede shoes, Matthew's brown sweater that brings out his eyes, Jessup's pair of running shorts I designed for him, and Carl's leather binder. It was all just another phantom ache in my soul, and I needed to get away, so the woods would be secluded and served a purpose.

Most people stay away from Ever Woods because of the moody little buggers that live here and control the emotional forest, but that's one thing I've always enjoyed and missed. That's the only thing I've missed about the Garden of Life. *Yeah, that's another thing they messed up on.* It was Life not fucking Eden. I digress. The thing is, I enjoyed the trees and animals that mingled around the creepy forest. It reminds me of home. It's a peaceful respite for me, due to the shadowy mist that wraps around me. It's as if they want to wrap their cool embrace around my colder heart. Thankfully, the moody bastards that made up the council seemed to always notice my presence and didn't try to fuck with me. *Smart of them.* I haven't had to set them straight in a few decades.

Walking along the worn-out path, I come to a sparsely shaded glade and decide to rest. Taking a seat on the cool outcrop of stones, I lean my head back and stretch out my chest. Ever since waking up, I have had a constant ache there that I can't relieve.

Crack!

Springing up off the rocks, my eyes search for the intruder that's daring to interrupt my peace.

"Relax, dear child." A soothing voice reaches me, but I still can't detect who's here. Hearing another stick snap behind me, I whirl around to see none other than Anwen standing there in her blue cloak. My body relaxes at the familiar Fate standing in front of me. She has not changed over the years; her ebony skin is still vibrating and has an ethereal glow. Her eyes are still a fascination to me—one purple with a white pentagram pupil, and the other black with a clock as its pupil.

For as long as I've been alive, there have always been three Fates. Their roles have always been a close secret and even though I'm a dear friend, I don't even know their *true* purpose. I do know that they were the ones that decided Purgatory would have schools where all Supernatural creatures were to attend. This had multiple reasons behind it: 1) this allowed the students to learn about the human world and allowed them to learn the magic that would help them adapt, and 2) it helped regulate the magic between the realms.

Anwen had once explained to me that if the magic became too powerful on one side of the realm, it started to pull and destroy the other side, so checks and balances needed to be made. The only place that wasn't affected as much was Hell, and I had smiled at that proclamation.

Before I met the guys, I was at my lowest. Nothing brought me pleasure anymore, and I was wandering around a small wooded area on the other side of the mountains, needing to get away from Hell when I first met Anwen. She approached me, and we talked for most of the day. It was kind of nice to chat, and she was able to pull me out of my bad mood and get my mind off of me for a change. I dare say we became friends that day. After a short time of getting to know each other, she told me that I wouldn't be alone for long, that I was destined to have mates. My first reaction was to scoff in her face.

Demons don't do the mate thing. Yes, we'd say that we have them, but it's just words. We don't feel that pull, have those deep feelings, and aren't able to have that eternal connection with someone. There had never been someone outside of Shifters that needed mates before, that I knew of. But after she stated that it was written in the stars for me to have not just one but multiple mates, I began to believe my new confidant. We often met up to just chat and gossip about my friends and her sisters. The females she considered her sisters were the other Fates; therefore, they all made up the powers that be.

Yes, I know how confusing this all is about Heaven, Hell, God, and now Fates, but I promise it's not that confusing living here.

"How are you, Anwen?" Greeting her with a small smile, I sit back down on the rock and take in her appearance. At first glance, all looks alright with her, but now taking in her form, I notice the hunch of her shoulders, her usually bright eyes have dimmed, and her hair has lost its usual luster.

"Dear child, I am sorry that you were taken and I could not come to you. I've missed you, but all is *not* well," she confesses, and tears gather in her eyes.

Oh no!

Rushing to her side and grabbing her arm gently, I guide her back to the rocks I was sitting on. Helping her down, I sit next to her and reach for her hand, lending her as much comfort as I can since I don't know what's going on.

"What's wrong? Are you sick?" It's very rare for a Fate to become sick. Last I heard, Anwen was looking for one of her sisters. *Shit!* That must be it. "Oh, I'm sorry. What happened to Liliwen? Did you ever find her?" I watch as her face falls even further if that's even possible.

"Yes," she sobs and leans into my side. Trying to offer her some comfort, I wrap my arms around her and bring her into an embrace. I hold her until her tears quietly run dry and her body stops shuddering. "I'm sorry, child. It's been years, and the heartache is still fresh," she confesses, wiping away her tears.

Taking in my confusion, she continues on. "Oh, I'm sorry. You don't know. Liliwen was found dead the day you were captured by Adam," she explains, and my heart drops at that confession. Little Liliwen was barely four foot tall, with long blonde hair and a slim frame. She reminded me of a child. The Fate of present transgressions was such a fair and soft-spoken lady. I will miss her. I didn't see much of her, but the times that I did, she brightened my day.

"I am so sorry to hear this. What happened, if you don't mind sharing?" Regret laces my voice as I wish there was something I could do to make things better. Because of Adam, I haven't been here to help Anwen and Seren mourn their lost sister, Liliwen. Anger boils underneath the surface as I think of how he tricked me into being captured. *How could I let down my defenses so easily?* Anwen sighs, pulling my morose thoughts back to her.

"Unfortunately, there isn't much to the story. She went missing, as you already know, and her body was found in one of the streams, drained of magic." She sighs as her shoulders drop slightly, but she pulls herself up to her full height as my arm slips away from her.

"What does that mean? Her magic was drained from her?" I wonder out loud. She didn't mention that her magic passed on to a new Fate, rather it was drained. *Odd.*

"Just what I said. Her magic was drained, but for what purpose, I have no clue. A new Fate will emerge soon, I feel it in my bones. But this is not why I sought you out." Anwen turns towards me and takes my hands into her warm touch. "I have come to warn you." Her words are barely above a whisper as her eyes take on a cloudy silver sheen over her already captivating pupils.

A breeze kicks up and rustles my hair, along with a few flower petals whipped up into the air. The sunlight that was once speckled around the glade has disappeared, leaving my skin pebbling as Anwen's grip tightens around my hands. She opens her mouth, but it's not her voice that speaks through her lips. It's as if multiple voices filter through her mouth when speaking of the prophecy. Don't ask me how I know that's what is about to happen. I just have a gut feeling since I trust her with my life. That's the only thing this could be.

"Four protectors bound in one soul,
Torn asunder through a hole.
Four souls split apart,
Tearing through a bleeding heart.
Climbing through the ranks of Hell,
The rebels you shall not repel.

Four young souls will embody thee.
To save us all, she will be the key.
Thy body will encompass true evil's hate,
When gone for long without thy mates.

Win them back for true loves power,
To tackle thy battle of the twelfth hour.
These tasks you must complete,
Or else, all will be obsolete."

Her voice floats away on the breeze as the wind settles and the sun pokes out behind the clouds. Anwen collapses as the tension rushes out of her body, and I easily catch her as she comes to.

Blinking rapidly to clear her eyes, she glances up at me and grabs my face in her palms. "Dear child, I am sorry this has befallen you," she sobs, while I'm lost trying to figure out the meaning of her prophecy. Who're the young souls? Are those my men? What did she mean by true evil's hate? That's the only thing which seemed to scream it was about me.

"Do you know what it means? Can you give me any guidance?" I plead with her, completely lost.

She slowly shakes her head and releases my cheeks in exchange for my hands once again. "The only thing I can tell you is that you need to get your mates back, or else your defenses will shatter." Squinting her eyes, they turn opaque once again as her gaze takes in my form for a moment before clearing again and going wide with shock. "It looks as if your defenses have already been weakened by the look of you. But all is not lost, child. You *must* get them back."

I nod my head, "Yes. Yes, they have. I'm po—" my throat closes once again as I'm silenced from trying to get help. Anwen's eyes soften as she takes in my defeated form.

"I understand more than you know, my child, but I cannot interfere. There is hope," she encourages.

My eyes drift closed of their own accord as I silently try to calm my racing heart. Even though I'm friends with the Fates, there is still a lot I don't know. One thing for sure, though, is that their prophecies are never wrong. I'm not sure what else I need to do, but the most obvious task is finding my men and getting them back!

I feel Anwen release my hands and as I take a deep breath.

"I have faith in you, Lilith. Your task will not be an easy one, and the road will be long. Still, I know you will prevail," she whispers as her hands run over my closed eyes and down my face to cradle it lightly before pulling away. Opening my eyes to say thank you, I find nothing but the sparse glade in front of me. Disappointment falls over me as I look around, wondering where to go or how to continue. I hear a soft internal chime that signals an incoming message and a note appears out of blue smoke on the rock I'm resting on. Before I reach for it, Anwens's voice comes to me on a breeze. "Your heart has always been a compass."

Absently rubbing the ache in my chest, I wonder if she means figuratively or literally. Does she mean my heartache can lead me back to my mates? It's a possibility, I guess. How would that even work, though? Another ping comes in with another note, pulling me out of my ramblings. Opening both, I read:

I got Adam 2 talk.
-M
U gonna answer? Fine. Last known Loc... Washington State.
-Murmur the badass

Yes! I finally have a starting location, though I'm a little nervous about what truly happened when I was gone. But I'm ready to go find my mates!

CHAPTER 11
Bye, Bye, Bye

Jessup

Flipping over onto my side, I let out a sigh and try to relax my muscles for the fifth time tonight. It's hopeless though. I've been tossing and turning since I first laid down an hour ago. I roll onto my other side and let out another sigh. "What's wrong, Jessie?" Lily mumbles, half asleep as she turns towards me, her brown hair splayed across the pillow.

"Nothing, Lily, just go back to sleep. I'm gonna go for a run," I grunt out as I get out of bed. I just can't lay here any longer. Throwing on my sweatpants, I slip out of the bedroom, leaving behind my pregnant girlfriend. Flinching from the slight pinch in my chest, I rub the area thinking of the reason for it. Ever since Lilith denounced me, the pain has been there. Anytime I think of her, or my girlfriend, the pain radiates throughout my chest as a reminder that I'm fucking up. *But is it really my fault? She's the one that left me!*

Ever since the fateful night where she left us and tore my

heart from my chest, it's left a pit that just aches and throbs daily—more so when I think of her or someone else besides her. My mate bond is a constant reminder, but what else am I supposed to do when she threw me away like garbage?

I must admit, things didn't go well after my Timberwolf took over. Normally, when I shift we share the same mind space, but I completely lost control and blacked out. I awoke two weeks later with the guys surrounding my body, covered in blood and mud.

Once they heard I had gone feral from a few Shifters that tried to approach me, they came to my rescue. They managed to corral me and bring me to Earth with them. They decided it would be safer and it was another way to preserve our broken pride within the gossip circle. Who needed to be around peers knowing you've been rejected by your mate? Thankfully, Matthew contacted a trusted friend and they created powerful wards to help contain me to the wooded area of the property they bought, and I was able to tear through my rage without killing anyone.

Slipping silently through the house, I walk out to the back porch and find my sneakers on the low bench. Slipping them on, I catch movement in the woods behind our property and my wolf perks up. Sniffing the air, I take in the faint scent of what could only be described as...*mate! Lilith?* My keen eyesight focuses on the edge of the woods and I listen carefully for any sounds. The nocturnal animals are still moving around and the ambiance of the woods hasn't changed, so why am I on high alert? I start stretching as I continue to watch the edge of the woods.

There's no way it could be Lilith. After I shifted back into my human form, we all sat down and talked about our heart-break over the woman we loved. We all agreed that her leaving us was so unlike her, but how she touched on our insecurities was only a dig that she would do to those in the past. Even with the vicious way of ending things, we still had hope. So, we decided that we would live together so when Lilith pulled her head out of her ass, she didn't have to track us all down. It stayed like that for a few years until we had enough and we decided to travel the world and go to all the places we knew she wanted to visit. After that turned up with a big fat nothing, we took a portal to Hell to see if there were any hints as to her whereabouts. I know it seems silly, but after our period of mourning and waiting for her, we just wanted that closure before moving on. A decade was nothing to us immortals, so I think we were patient enough.

We searched everywhere for her but it was like she went and disappeared without a trace. L.A.M.B. was nowhere to be seen either. They were probably making their rounds on Earth too, so we couldn't question them about Lilith's whereabouts. It never occurred to us that she might not have wanted to be found. Deep down, I was hoping she would just take one look at us and demand to have us back. So after that fiasco, we decided to slowly work our way up to moving on.

The first thing we did was build four separate houses on the land we had bought when my Timberwolf took over, we just bought out the woods that surrounded the area. Then we started going on a few dates here and there over the years until just recently. I say we, but it's really everyone except Carl. He was adamant that it couldn't have been Lilith that broke our hearts. To this day, he's stuck by the memory of her like a faithful little dog. I love the guy, I really do, but for a genius, he really is naive. Lilith didn't care about ripping out our hearts and sucking the life from them. She got off on that shit.

The Fates must have had a hand in things with how we met our current love interests. We went out drinking about seven months ago at a local bar, just to get out of our houses. One of those nights to just blow off steam, play darts, and listen to the dive bar's live music. A group of four human women walked into the bar and sat down next to our table. One thing led to another and we all started talking. It turned out they were best friends and they wanted a girls night out. Except for Carl, each of us hooked up that night.

Who knew that one night would end up with us getting them pregnant by chance? But Carl became friendly enough with the younger one. Of course, we couldn't tell them what we were. If they knew, they probably would have run away screaming. It's something I've been putting off, but I'll have to tell her sooner rather than later because the child she's carrying will most likely be a Shifter also.

Finishing up my light stretching, I take off in a familiar loop around the border of our property to run some of the angst and steam out of my body. Hopefully, I can clear my head enough to power through another day.

Matthew

Leaning back in my chair, I sip at my tea, watching the light pinks of the early morning sunrise peek over the eastern mountains. It's peaceful in this secluded section of our paradise together. Lilith would have loved this, even though she was made for city life. She was so eccentric and thrived with people. I enjoy the simple life, it also helps that I'm not around all of the hustle and bustle, otherwise I have to constantly block people out and hold my mental shields tight.

In other words, I've been lazy, but what else do you expect, we've been on vacation. We have ten more years here before we have to go back to Purgatory to step into the roles we've been selected for.

Jessup makes his final lap and slows down to a walk as he approaches the back deck of my bungalow. "Couldn't sleep again?" I inquire. He's been more restless than normal lately.

"Yeah."

He starts stretching as we both enjoy the comfortable silence. I wonder what's really going on with him because he's been on edge more than anything. I wonder if it's the fact we're on Earth, or if it's the babies that are getting closer to their due dates. We had to take a 'guys' weekend a month ago just to get him out and run his aggression into the ground. Daniel and him sparred for hours until both of them dropped from exhaustion. I think we all needed it, to be honest. It's been stressful lately, with all of us being on the fence about what to tell our girlfriends, if anything, about us being supernatural creatures. Jessup has been taking it harder than the rest of us, warring back and forth between keeping quiet or having full disclosure.

Carl is completely against it because he still believes Lilith didn't leave us. Though, that didn't stop him from trying to have a child like the rest of us. He wanted his child to grow up with the rest of ours, yet I bet he didn't go about it the conventional way. I'm curious as to how he actually did it while still being faithful to Lilith. He wanted to be faithful no matter what.

Jessup was on the fence about the whole thing since Lily would more or less leave him. She was very religious oriented and didn't believe in anything occult related. Lanna, Daniel's girl, was all about the occult. Even though she's well into her twenties, she still dresses like the typical goth schoolgirl trying to find herself. Of course, that causes issues in their relationship since Daniel is vying for a senate seat and has an image to keep. I can't tell you how much resentment I catch rolling off of them. That's a recipe for disaster. One of them has to give a little to make that work. I'm surprised it worked out for this long. I'm sure the only reason they are together is that she's expecting a little Vamp herself. Though, she doesn't know that part.

Cocking his head to the side, Jessup freezes and listens for a moment before sitting down on the edge of the deck with me. "Layla's up," he announces.

Nodding my head that I heard him, I take another sip of my tea, finishing it up before answering. "She'll be busy with her morning routine. Want to talk about it?" I nonchalantly question, placing my cup down on the end table as I change the subject. He's not one to be pressured into talking, but I'm hoping he's finally at the point of opening up a little bit. He throws his feet out in front of him and bends over to stretch out his legs. I wait patiently as his feelings war within him until he settles on resignation.

"I don't know what the right answer is, Caldron. Every time I think about coming forward with Lily, I get this sharp——"

"Pain in your chest," I interrupt him as I rub at the same spot he's absent-mindedly rubbing.

"Yeah," he admits. "I think it's from Lilith, our bond, and I don't know what it means. It's been getting stronger and more frequent lately."

"Maybe we should get the guys together tonight and see if they're experiencing the same things," I suggest. We haven't had a guys night in a while, so it's about time anyway.

"I doubt Dan will be down for it," Jessup growls out and stands up, looking over my shoulder. I know he's sensing Layla in the kitchen, probably making hotcakes before I have to go to work.

It's her way of trying to make up for the fact that she's cheating on me. Though, can you really cheat on someone when you're only with them because they got pregnant from a one-night stand? She tries her best to make it work between us, but the fire isn't there. It doesn't help that I can read her feelings that she's not happy with me like she's yelling in my face. She's having an affair with her boss and is convinced she's in love with him. A few times, I've noticed that she's not happy with the idea of being a mother and that might work for me in the long run. I might be able to have her sign over rights and let her go off and live the life she wants.

"Don't worry about Daniel. I know what to say to get him hooked and wanting to join us for some guy time," I say while I pull out a stack of post-it notes and a pen from the pocket inside of my chair. I quickly scribble out two notes inviting everyone to poker tonight at 9pm and lay them in the palm of my hand. With a puff of air, they go up in green smoke. Feeling my pockets in my pants getting heavier instantaneously makes me smile as I pull out their responding notes.

We really needed to get a handle on these cell phone devices that are becoming the new rave. We all have them, but it's taking us forever to get the handle on them. We simply have them for the girls and emergencies, but we mostly rely on our magic to communicate between all of us.

"We're on for tonight, just meet up at our normal spot," I say and wiggle my eyebrows at Jessup, making him laugh. He waves as he takes off around the corner and back to his house. Maybe we can work this shit out tonight. If anything, maybe it will help confirm I'm not the only one going crazy with this phantom pain.

CHAPTER 12
Moody Women

Daniel

Clomp, clomp, clomp! I swear you would think I was living with a herd of elephants, but unfortunately, it's just Lanna stomping around. Slipping a small pack of post-it notes and pen back in my pocket after replying to Mattie, I glance up and find Lanna at the top of the stairs. She stomps down the stairs with her blocky black boots, black jeans, a flowy black tank top protruding over her swollen belly, and a suitcase dragging behind her. *Not this again! She's driving me crazy to the point of despising the thought of her, but I can't let her leave carrying my heir.*

"Where are you going now?" I sigh in defeat. There's always some kind of drama with this woman.

"Well, since you're so busy with work and you're never here, I figured I would do better on my own," she pouts. Talk about being dramatic, she would give the damn Brownies a run for their money when they didn't have anything to fucking clean.

"Well, how about we do this? I have to meet with the guys

70

tonight, so let me book you a massage and then tomorrow you can have a girls' day here at the house. I can have caterers come in and spoil you and your friends. Deal?"

She reaches me and crosses her arms under her breasts, lifting those big cans for my inspection. She knows how much I enjoy nice breasts, and before I can think of anything else, a jolt of pain hits me in the chest, right where my dead heart lies. *FUCK! This shit is getting annoying.*

I wince but easily turn it into a quirk, waiting for her answer. "Does that sound okay?" I ask again and give her an impatient look.

"Fine! But can you book a pedicure too? My feet are killing me," she says, turning and gliding on soft feet into the living room, leaving her suitcase in the middle of the entrance hall. *Well, maybe if you didn't wear such hideous shoes, they wouldn't hurt!*

Taking her suitcase, I fly up the stairs with my Vampire speed and go to her room down the hall. Yes, she has shared my bed a few times while I was drowning out my sorrow, but she has her own room for her own protection because I've come close to strangling the spoiled brat. I know I haven't helped with turning around and giving her whatever she wants, but I'm tired of all this. Everything was perfect in the beginning like most shallow relationships. Young, vibrant, hot blonde with big tits, something wet to put my dick in and try to get over Lilith, but the more Lanna got comfortable with me, the more she changed. After the first night that she got pregnant, I was stuck and couldn't very well get rid of her, so what else was I supposed to do?

First her hair, then her clothes, the idea of blood play I was down for, but then the attitude and snippiness. It was just too much at times. Throwing her case on the bed and opening it, I find it empty. Grinding my teeth together, I close my eyes for a brief second to try and calm my anger. Fuck this! I need an outlet and if I touch Lanna right now, she might not live long enough to give birth to my child.

Leaving her empty suitcase on the bed, I quickly go down the hall and into my bathroom, turning the shower to scorching. Slipping out of my sweaty workout clothes, I quickly step under the hot stream.

In the past, when I got angry it was for a good reason, well maybe not a good one, but I at least enjoyed the way we made up. Angry sex is the best if you're with someone that knows how to push your buttons and then cool you off. Lilith never shied away from the rough and dirty; she reveled in it. Hell, we spent years fucking over dead corpses and tortured souls that were locked in Iridium cages. *I miss those days. She was perfect. My perfect woman.*

With frustration coursing through my body, I quickly wash and rinse my hair. Grabbing the body wash I start washing my body but my mind keeps wandering back to the last time I enjoyed a shower in this state. I had been worked up just like I am now, but instead of hoping the heat and water pressure would miraculously resolve my tension, I had a beautiful woman kneeling in front of me. Just thinking about Lilith covered with soap suds barely covering her rosey pink nipples has blood rushing to my cock.

No. I'm not doing this. My hands slowly glide over my chest and stomach as I try to pull out of the memory. I seem to spend most of my time either working out or taking long showers to help alleviate the tension in my body. I was debating adding another hot water heater just so I wouldn't have to worry about running out of scalding water. I can't help but laugh at the idea. The last time I added water heaters was when Lilith and I wanted to perform some sexathons in our shower. Having the water rush over us as our bodies were pressed together makes my cock bob for attention.

Dammit.

Leaning my head against the wall, the water cascades down my back and it feels like the lingering touches Lilith used to leave before she crawled out of bed. Or the feather light touches she gave me while she was below me and was about to take my shaft into her small, manicured hands.

My right hand slowly trails down my stomach and over my chiseled abs until I reach my cock standing at attention. *Damn you, Lilith, for leaving me.* Taking my length in my hand, I close my eyes and imagine it's Lilith's small hand wrapped firmly around it instead of my own. Her bright blue eyes piercing mine with a glint shining out, signaling her mischievous side wants to play. She often liked to play and see how she could prolong my orgasm with those dick-sucking lips of hers. She was a force to be reckoned with.

Smirking, she kneels down between my legs and licks her lips before taking me down her throat. Squeezing the base of my cock, she bobs up and down on my shaft moaning. Pulling off my cock, she runs her tongue over my head causing me to moan as she licks up the precum dripping from my slit. *Damn! It's been so long, Lilith!*

Looking down, I imagine her smirk at hearing her name on my lips before taking me into her hot mouth again and increasing her speed. My hips start to pump in and out of her mouth in a frenzy as my abs contract and pressure builds. Reaching down to fondle my sack, Lilith takes me all the way back down her throat and swallows and it sends me over the edge, moaning Lilith's name. Hot ropes of cum paint my shower floor before it's washed away.

Fuck!

Leaning up against the shower wall, all I can think of is that no one can compare to Lilith.

Carl

Walking back to the front door, I catch Lucy glancing my way from the corner of my eye and I internally sigh. I knew it was a mistake to offer my services for the ladies' pregnancies, but I couldn't let them go to a *human* hospital knowing the babies they were carrying weren't human. Nope, they were all Supes, and powerful ones at that, in their own right. Instead of taking them to the clinic, like I wanted to, the guys talked me into seeing the ladies here at my house. How in the Fates name did I allow *that* to happen?

Simple.

It was common sense. I had the knowledge and space in my house. I even had the equipment in the office I had built in the back of my house for just this reason.

So not only did I have to see Lucy all the time, she was in my home. Alone. With. Me.

How awkward. It seemed I was always fighting off her advancements. If I wasn't convinced that Lilith wasn't the one that broke up with me, then I might have indulged in what the guys were trying to do. But I know in my heart that Lilith didn't leave us, I just don't know what happened or where she's at. At the thought of Lilith, a stabbing pain punctures my soul and I try to catch my breath.

Damn, these are getting stronger.

"You know, Carl, I've noticed you're alone a lot. Doesn't your girlfriend live with you?"

"I've asked you to call me Dr. Steinbeck," I mutter out, but Lucy still continues.

"I've been around for what, seven months now, and have yet to meet the woman I'm supposedly carrying your baby for?" Lucy inquires once again. It's been the same thing every time I've had to do a check-up. Thank the Fates I didn't actually sleep with this woman. She would be attached to my dick, and that would be awkward to walk around with all day.

Turning to face her, I paste what I hope is a friendly smile on my face, hopefully hiding the annoyance I feel.

"Miss Lacroix. I appreciate you and all that you have done to help bring a child into this world, but like I've said before, my personal business is my own."

Instead of following me to the front door, Lucy veers off and sits down in my living room. Taking a moment to bow my head and letting out a deep breath, I calm down a bit before following her.

"She's beautiful," Lucy states, picking up the picture of Lilith and I that was taken the day before she broke all of our hearts. "But we both know she's not around," she smirks up at me.

My stomach flips with unease for a moment. Is everything I worked so hard for about to fall apart? Why can't she just take the money I'm throwing at her and be happy? I know she wants to feel the same way as her best friends do, but my heart isn't in it. Hell, from what the guys have all said, even her friends aren't happy. So that's why I came up with the idea of paying her to be a surrogate.

Humans would probably call me a mad scientist if they knew what I was capable of. In Purgatory, it was encouraged to experiment and expand new horizons. Since Lilith couldn't conceive or carry a child, I had taken one of her eggs and figured out how to infuse her essence into it along with my own sperm. It helps having the type of magic that attunes to what I need. It was all a theory when we were in Purgatory, but we had all talked about having kids this way once we got married.

On many occasions Lilith and I had discussed different ways to possibly have kids since she was barren. She was cursed with infertility when she was cast out as Adam's first wife. So, a few years before we were slated to come to Earth, we experimented on pulling her essence and making children that way. So of course, when we came to Earth, I brought her frozen egg with me in hopes that she would change her mind and we could carry out our plan. Or maybe it was a part of me that just wanted a piece of her by my side. Either way, I was glad I had brought it because it was only when the guys announced they messed up and got the other women pregnant, that the idea of using Lucy even occurred to me. I haven't even told the guys what I've done. I'm sure they think I used Lucy's eggs to have a child.

I'll have to straighten that out with them soon.

Maybe I made the mistake in not explaining all the science to Lucy and how surrogates work. She probably thinks she's carrying 'our' child, which is the furthest thing from the truth. Either way, she signed all the proper documents, Daniel's lawyers looked over them, and she's getting more money than a Fortune 500 business.

Before I can retort, a soothing balm hits my chest as a musical voice filters in behind me.

CHAPTER 13

Here I come, ready or not

Lilith

Looking through the kitchen window, I can't help but wonder who the pregnant woman is that's causing Carl distress. She doesn't look like a lover, more like someone that needed a firm hand, especially if I had anything to do with it. I finally found my mates a couple of days ago. I probably would have found them sooner if it hadn't been for the damned Demons inside of me fucking things up. I would blackout and find myself a hundred miles away from my original starting point. Thankfully, they can't control me all of the time; they would probably need another two or three stuffed into my head to have enough control for that. I was more than determined to find my mates though, inconvenience or not. But from what I can tell, the rumors were true. My men have moved on without me, all except Carl. The only question I have right now is why.

'So you can see him move on without you in person. There's no reason to go in and see him,' the guttural voice—Rocks —hisses out.

I had come to the realization that even though they weren't the smartest Demons to possess me, they did have some type of self-preservation since they wouldn't tell me their names. So I've come to name them myself.

'Yes. He's clearly busy with his new lover,' the squeaky voice Demon—Chew Toy—laughs.

'This is boring, let's go,' the serious voice—Grumpy —whines.

I suppress a growl at their comments and watch my mate.

Anwen was one sneaky Fate. When she had said, 'my heart was a compass,' she wasn't joking. Once I made it here to Washington, it was only a matter of time—and a matter of following the pains in my chest—until I found them. Turns out the stronger they were, the closer I was to finding them. And finding them, I did. And this woman, pregnant or not, is making my prince uncomfortable, and I can't have that.

My first instinct when I saw my mates again was to show them why you didn't cross the Queen of Hell. But after observing them for a time, they didn't seem as happy as they presented themselves to the world. Their lovers obviously didn't know about their abilities. From what I saw, Jessup doesn't shapeshift and run amuck even with their houses being this secluded. Daniel doesn't seem to sleep, and he's been spending his days either working out or showering, by himself I might add.

Matthew is the only one that appears somewhat content, but that might have been because he wasn't surrounded by Supes always trying to use him for his abilities or having to constantly shield himself. Carl looks downright miserable, but not once do I doubt his loyalty. He has turned his house into a shrine of me. Pictures of us litter his dwelling, and it warms my black heart immensely. If anyone can give me answers and help put this puzzle together, it will be him.

Slipping into the house through the back door, I glide up

the stairs and hear the harlot mention how she knows I'm not around, and it brings me such pleasure to know I'm about to ruin her day.

"Oh. There you are, honey," I say in my most flattering voice. I like to call it my death-by-sugar voice.

Carl whips around so fast, almost knocking off his glasses, and freezes as he takes me in. He looks at me as if I've just floated down from Heaven, or in truth, just risen from Hell. Either way, it makes me feel like the goddess I know I am.

Our little moment is broken by a shriek. "Who's this?" the young lady sitting on Carl's sofa asks.

On the softest whisper that only I can hear, Carl says, "My mate." Again, he makes my heart soar as I send him a smile worthy of a cover shoot. I wonder for the first time if hearts are capable of just floating away with so much love.

'Love is overrated. He left you to rot in Hell, remember?' Grumpy says.

Stepping into his arms is like coming home. The ache in my chest soothes just a little, but the tiny ache reminds me that I'm not complete, not yet. "We need to talk, but it seems you have company."

Pulling away from our embrace, Carl gives me a small smile and nods, but not before giving me a small kiss. His lips are as soft as I remember. "Yes, dear. Trust me and I'll explain everything," he whispers and turns around, grabbing my hand to address the woman trying to take my place.

"Oh, Lucy! Sorry about my manners, let me correct that. This is Lilith, my girlfriend," he begins, and I bite my tongue so I don't blurt out that we are more than just that simple term. He pulls our combined hands up to his lips and presses a sweet kiss along my knuckles as I maintain a sweet and neutral look. "And Lilith, this is our surrogate, Lucy. She's the one that's carrying our child. I just finished her checkup when she asked about you. Both are healthy as can be."

The breath is kicked out of me as my body sways a bit from the news. Thankfully no one notices, and I'm quick to suppress my look of shock.

Our child? Did he really carry on what we were talking about after all this time?

I quickly observe Lucy's reaction to Carl's introduction and can easily tell she was *not* expecting that as an answer, even though my pictures are plastered around the room. I slide on a smile and approach the poor woman, pulling her up off the sofa and into a quick hug.

"Lucy! It's such a pleasure to finally meet you. Carl has told me so much about you. And thank you so much, from the bottom of my heart, for doing this for us. It's been a dream of ours for the longest time." I gently lead her towards the front door where I restrain myself from slamming her into it head first. "It's such a relief to know that you are both healthy and doing well, but I'll have to cut our meeting short. I wasn't expecting Carl to have a guest, and I must get him ready for another meeting that we absolutely can't be late for," I say as I open the front door. "But don't worry, I'll be sure to check in with you soon," I say and watch as a dazed Lucy walks out the door and down to her car.

"I see you still enjoy threatening mortals." Carl comes up behind me and wraps his arms around my waist, calming down my internal ire.

"I do enjoy that pastime," I confess, turning in his arms and wrapping mine around his neck and kicking his front door shut as I hear Lucy's car door slam.

Carl doesn't even give me a moment to catch my breath or demand answers before slamming his mouth to mine, devouring me. It's as if he's been in a desert for the past ten years and he finally gets to have a sip of water, but he can't just stop there. No. I'm never enough for my eager Carl, and it's just the way I want it. Losing myself in his arms once again, I forget about all his trespasses as he leads us back down the hall to his bedroom.

I claw at his button up shirt, ripping it down the middle as I kick off my heels. Carl pulls my shirt over my head and pulls down the cups of my black lace bra, exposing my taut nipples. Reaching down, he pulls one into his waiting mouth and sucks it greedily, causing mewling sounds to fall from my lips. Tiny pulses fly straight to my clit, demanding attention where I need it the most. I crave him as much as I need my next breath, but I'm still pissed that he up and fucking left me. Not once did he fucking look for me.

"I want to feel you inside me, but I think you need to earn it first," I heave out between heavy breaths.

Carl quickly undoes my bra and asks, "What do you mean?" before lavishing kisses over my chest and rolling my other nipple between his fingers, then swiftly taking that one into his mouth and biting gently.

Any other time I would be glad to have Carl attached to my nipples like a little barnacle, but I think before I can relish my time with him, I need to dish out some punishment.

"It's been over a decade, Carl," I purr, running my hands through his short black hair.

He replies with a muffled, "Mmmhmm." And twirls his tongue around my nipple. Suppressing a moan, I dig my nails into his hair and yank his head back, making his teeth graze across my sensitive peak. I snap my fingers, relieving us of our clothes. Without my clothes, my arousal starts to ease down my inner thighs. "A decade since I've ridden this cock." I reach down and squeeze the base of his dick and slowly stroke him before collecting his precum on the tip of my finger. "Or tasted your cum." I bring my finger up to his lips and he opens for me, licking his cum clean from my finger. "Does it taste as good as I remember?" His reply is to lick his lips.

Reaching down, I gather my evidence of arousal on my

fingertips and bring it to my lips, about to take a lick when Carl pouts. My grown Fae prince pouts that he can't taste me on his tongue. That realization brings a smile to my face as I pull harder on his hair and he grunts. "It's been a decade since you've licked me clean, Carl. My dear sweet prince. Do I taste as good as you remember?" I ask, as I watch his tongue dart out and try to lick my fingers that are just out of reach.

"Please, Lilith. I need to taste you."

"You always know what to say to make me happy," I murmur and run my fingers along his tongue as he moans and praises me.

As I release some of the tension on his hair, his heated gaze lands on me once again.

"Would you like that? To lick me clean?" I tease, his Adam's apple bobbing up and down as he swallows.

"Yes, my queen," he chokes out.

"Good." I lean in, kissing him passionately and then biting him semi-hard on his full bottom lip and snap my fingers again.

I move over to the bed and look down at my lover where I magicked him. Carl's now lying supine with a blindfold over his eyes and his wrists and ankles are tied to the bed. The gray and white bedding matched well with his custom black metal bed frame with science beakers for the posts. I've always loved having beds with these kinds of head and footboards. You could do so many wonderful things with them.

"Lilith," Carl chokes out. "You know I hate being blind-folded." A tinge of fear rises in his voice and that little sick part of my mind revels in it.

"Oh, really? I must have forgotten your little quirks while I wasted away in the seventh level of Hell for three months."

"Tha...that's where you were?" Carl manages to get out, tensing with the realization.

He looks perfect there all spread out along his bed like a

buffet for me to enjoy. The speckling of fine hair on his chest and the happy trail leading down to his proud and straining cock does things to me. He really is the perfect Fae male specimen. I'm so lucky that the Fae women from his court are missing out, but first, I need to teach my little prince that no matter what comes between us, he shouldn't have left me to rot in the bowels of Hell.

"Yes." I crawl up onto the bed and position myself, straddling his covered eyes with the view of his bobbing cock in front of me with a riding crop in my hand.

Having magic does have its benefits. Especially when punishing my men.

"I had an Iridium dagger shoved into my back and was thrown behind bars while my *mates*—" swat at his dick "—played house," I growl out. Smiling as he moans with the contact, I continue as I run the leather across his balls. "I was finally found by L.A.M.B. Imagine my surprise when they told me, my *mates*—" another whack to his cock "—had moved on without me."

"Lilith," Carl moans in pleasure, "it's not..." his muffled excuse trails off as he gets a mouth full of my pussy.

"Enough! It's time to pay homage to your queen, and then, if you've satisfied me, I might listen to your pitiful pleas to explain your insolence," I demand, grinding my pussy against his waiting tongue. Damn, how I've missed his mouth. Not only did he speak of eloquent science equations, but also his tongue was magic.

Carl quickly starts devouring my pussy like a man digging for lost treasure, and it's so good it makes my eyes roll back. "Mmm. Yes, just like that." It's almost a shame that I tied his hands but then again if I hadn't, he wouldn't let me use my prop.

I'm stuck in a fascinating trance, watching as slight tremors wrack his body from the leather crop tracing over him. He pulls my needy clit into his mouth and sucks hard, causing me to lose my concentration for a moment. I reach up and play with my nipple as I roll my hips and buck against Carl's needy lips. He growls, wanting more so I tilt my hips so my clit is back within his reach. I'm so close to the edge that when he sucks hard on my bundle of nerves, lightning races through my body and I explode on his lips.

My legs shake and quiver as he continues to lap up my cream, and I watch as precum dribbles down his shaft. Leaning forward, I greedily lick up my appetizer and savor his delicious salty taste. His dick bobs up and down as I tease him with a few licks before taking him deep into my mouth. I moan around his cock and I feel his body tremble underneath me.

"Now that I've had my appetizer, let's have some real fun. Shall we, my prince?"

As soon as I move off of him, I use my magic to untie his legs and remove his blindfold.

"Damnit, Lilith. You know I'm not into that kind of stuff," he says, as his eyebrows pull down, and his lips thin with hard eyes, not hiding his ire.

"I know, and that's why it's part of your punishment," I say, straddling his hard cock. It's amazing how fast his emotions change once he sees my new position.

"May I dare ask what the other part of my punishment is?" Carl asks with a whimsical look. It's as if he's looking forward to this as I let my tail out to play.

"You get to be my sex toy. I'm going to get myself off on this wonderful, thick cock of yours. Then, you're going to tell me what happened from your perspective. Only when I'm satisfied with your answers will I forgive you and let you come," I state as I slide my hand between us to guide his cock to my wet folds.

His face falls at my confession before his eyes roll back as I slide down his shaft with a moan. *He still fits just like a puzzle piece.*

"Fuck. I've missed you so much. Yeah, like that! Ride my cock," he groans beneath me. Damn, I love the sound of his husky voice.

Picking up my pace, I grind my hips in circles as the end of my tail gently wraps around his balls. While my tail gently pulls and caresses his most sensitive area, I watch with a salacious smile as his legs jerk and he subconsciously pulls at the binds around his wrists to stop me. I'm not inflicting torture like I do with most of my victims, but knowing he's experiencing a little pain along with the pleasure makes my body tingle with glee.

A warmth I know all too well starts to fill my core as I allow my head to fall back and take in the sensations. It's a clash of heat and chills that rush up and down my body, hardening my nipples until they ache to be touched. Carl's eyes glaze over slightly as he watches me squeeze and play with my breasts while moans and heavy breathing are pulled from my lips as pleasure courses through me.

Gliding my hands up his flat stomach, I admire how he's never felt the need to become ripped to fit in. He's always felt comfortable with his brains rather than brawn.

"God, Lilith, your pussy is choking my cock so well."

With every circle of my hips, his lips twitch and his fists clench. My prince is getting close. *Should I let him come with me? I'm so close.*

"Make me see stars and you can come with me," I pant, snapping my fingers and releasing his hands.

He immediately grabs my hip with one hand, hard enough to bruise and thrusts up, controlling our pace. "Harder," I moan, and he wastes no time fulfilling my request. His other hand snakes up my thigh before his thumb circles my clit, sending me spiraling into the heavens. I'm lightheaded; my body locks up as I spasm around his cock and stars explode behind my eyelids as I close them.

I continue to slowly grind my hips against Carl as he begs in his Fae language for a release. Grabbing his throat, I pull him to me, tasting my musk on his lips as I slam my mouth to his.

"Come. For. Me. Prince," I pant with each thrust of his hips.

He furiously pumps into me a few more times before he finds his release with a moan. His dick pulses a few times before he lets out a sigh, blinking roughly, and looks up at me. "I love you, my dear, and I'm so glad you came back to me." Without waiting for a response, he wraps his arms around me and pulls me down onto his chest.

I roll so I'm on my side and entwine our legs together. Looking up into his dark brown eyes, I decide to clear up some things. I am beyond confused, and even though this reunion went a lot better than I expected, I still need answers.

"Carl, tell me what happened after you left me sleeping the day before we were supposed to go to Earth. I'm pretty sure we might have two different stories."

CHAPTER 14
Boys will be boys

Matthew

I need to get my shit under control, and quickly. The guys are going to be here any minute and I was the one that called this meeting. I have no idea why I'm nervous. The only thing I can think of is this constant hole in my chest and the flares which I think are a resemblance of Lilith's familiar feelings, but that can't be right. *She told us to fuck off over a decade ago, so why am I picking up on random feelings of love and longing now?*

I grab the bottle of Fae wine and pour myself a small amount, sipping it before I end up downing it in one go to calm my nerves. As I set down the glass and debate pouring another one, the door opens to our small cabin and Daniel walks in and immediately starts undoing his tie.

"Long day?" I ask, immediately reaching for the bourbon and pouring him a glass. Anger rolls off of him in waves and I pull my shields shut a little tighter to keep a headache from starting tonight.

"You have no idea," he says, accepting the drink.

I pour two more drinks for the rest of the guys and bring them over to the poker table where Daniel makes himself comfortable. This was the first building on the property before we built our own separate houses. This little cabin is our home away from home, and we often use it to get away from the women when we need a break. In most cases, it's where we can let out our otherness without the worry of being caught. Daniel can drink his blood or hunt animals, Jessup can shift, Carl can practice his magic if he wants, and I work spells so I won't be rusty. Carl and I have decent-sized workrooms, and there's a fighting ring outside for Daniel and Jessup to work out their angst. The perimeter is spelled to repel anyone not welcomed, so we don't have to worry about uninvited guests accidentally wandering into our sanctuary. And the aerial view is spelled to look like the rest of the woods that surround the area.

"Thank fuck we're having this meeting," Jessup says by way of a greeting.

He takes a look at the drinks on the table before marching over to the bar and grabbing the bottle of bourbon. Well, I guess I misjudged how stressed we've all been lately. I take my seat and look around, noticing we're missing Carl. "Where's Steinbeck?"

"Right here. Sorry for running late," he says, rushing through the door. He straightens his shirt and slides on his glasses before he looks up and gives us the goofiest smile I've seen on his face in years.

What the fuck is going on? If I didn't know better, I would say he just got laid.

He walks over and sits down next to Jessup and places his hands in his lap as if they can hold in the excitement that's pouring off of him. He reminds me of a child in a candy shop that's just waiting for the green light to go on a shopping spree for all the candy he can carry.

"What's got into you?" Daniel questions Carl as he looks at his phone before turning it off in a huff.

Picking up the drink in front of him, Jessup's nose flares when he brings it up to smell, and his eyes go wide. The glass topples, spilling its contents as Jessup drops it in exchange for Carl's collar.

In the blink of an eye, Carl is underneath a half-shifted Jessup with claws digging into his shirt and fangs millimeters away from his face. "How the fuck is that possible?"

Shit! I don't know what's going on, but this definitely isn't what was supposed to happen tonight. I reach for Carl as Daniel comes over and helps to pull Jessup off of our friend. "Jessup, you have to let him up. He can't talk when you're seconds away from ripping out his throat," he reminds him.

Who knew logic would actually work? Carl scrambles up off the floor with my help, his smile long gone, and retreats to the bar. He pours himself a shaky glass of Fae wine and takes a sip. Glancing over, I see Daniel with scrunched eyebrows and thin lips. I can see Jessup shaking as his muscles spasm, and his jaw clenches while he tries to control himself. He's about to explode if Carl doesn't say something soon.

"You better start talking right this fucking moment, Carl, before I lose my shit and I'm down one friend," Jessup chokes out.

Carl blanches and tosses back the drink, then throws up his hands as he clears his throat and stares Jessup in the eye. "Okay, I'll explain, but you have to promise me—no—you will *listen* to everything I have to say without interrupting or doing anything stupid. Actually, that applies to all of you." He waves a hand at the other two of us, and my brow furrows in annoyance, but I let it go. *If anyone can keep things together, it's me; all thanks to the tutelage of Lil*—I cut off that line of thinking and focus back on the other men.

"Okay, but hand over more alcohol before you get started." Jessup's eyes flash as he holds out his hand for Carl to pass over more drinks.

Shit, I know we're here to talk about Lilith, but I didn't expect it to be this explosive so soon. I don't think I'm emotionally ready to deal with this shit, but bring it on.

CHAPTER 15

Confessions
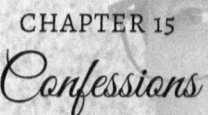

Carl

I walked into this cabin in such high spirits that I didn't even think about what would happen when Jessup caught Lilith's scent. Thankfully he wasn't so far gone that he ripped me to pieces. I was reluctant to fight him mainly because I'm a little rusty on the offensive magic. I need to make a note to schedule some time and practice.

But my first priority is getting our family back together, so as the guys get comfortable I lean against the bar, using it as a makeshift shield. I was caught off guard a moment ago, but I won't be making that mistake again.

Stealing myself with a deep breath, I make sure I have all of their attention and I dive in by breaking the news that Lilith is back and explaining what Lilith told me about being tricked and imprisoned. Outrage pours out with that news. Everyone here has met Lilith's ex-husband, and none of us would piss on him to save him if he was on fire. Jessup blows up, flipping a chair, and needs a few minutes to clear his head before we continue so as he walks around the cabin; we sit in silence.

Matthew yells profanities before clenching his fist and closing his eyes to take in deep breaths. Afterward, he slowly sips on his drink as his muscles ripple under his jacket. After Daniel's fist runs through the drywall, he quietly flips a poker chip as he stares off into space. Once Jessup comes back, we all take a few minutes to debate how Adam went about tricking *us* into thinking it was Lilith and we all came up with blank ideas. On one hand, they are all relieved, but on the other, emotions are high and they are still pissed—more at themselves than anything if I have to guess.

I explain how L.A.M.B. saved her from the seventh level of Hell, pulled the God-blessed dagger from her back, and how she had to recover and miss more days without us. This time, Matthew is the only one that reacts as tears gather in his eyes. Daniel is as stoic as a fucking statue, and Jessup just squints as if he's wondering if he should buy the story or not. I know it's a lot that I'm laying on them, so before they can ask any questions, I explain how she found us and the theory that the pain in our chest is from our broken bond this entire time.

"So that's why we were having the pains in our chest and it's probably the reason you still have them. It was the bond telling us it was broken and it was how Lilith was able to find us once she got to Earth. My bond is fixed, so I don't feel the pain anymore. Since you guys are in relationships, Lilith didn't come here with me even though I assured her you would want to see her," I tell them.

"How is yours fixed?" Jessup asks skeptically.

Heat rushes up to my cheeks as I blush and clear my throat. "Well, we just had to consummate our bond once again," I say with a smirk.

"That explains the look that was on your face," Matthew mumbles.

"Yeah, sorry," I reply, dropping my eyes in embarrassment for a moment.

I observe the room as everyone leans back in their chairs with differing looks of awe and disbelief. Matthew looks completely devastated, and I don't need to be a genius to know that he's questioning their last interaction. He's dissecting every word, the body language, and the reactions that they had. Jessup's brows are pulled together, reflecting his worry as he stands up and starts pacing back and forth. Daniel makes eye contact with me from across the room.

"Whe...Where is she now?" Daniel manages to get out. He remained seated throughout my explanation—except for the fist through the wall. Though he fidgeted; he either played with a toothpick, flipped poker chips, or shuffled cards.

"She's in the lab working on something for you guys. She said she would *try* to be patient and give you all the weekend to figure out what you will do to earn her forgiveness, but as you know, she's not a patient being," I say with a dreamy look on my face. My thoughts drift back to all the things that she made me do to earn her forgiveness.

"What was your punishment?" Matthew asks with a raised brow. My cheeks heat while I take off my glasses and clear my throat.

"All of the things I hate in the bedroom," I admit.

"Still hate to be blindfolded, huh?" Jessup stops pacing and gives me a smug look.

"Yes," I reply, curling my lip.

The screech of a chair pulls my attention back to Daniel standing up from the table. "Well, all I know is Carl got off scot free since he always believed Lilith didn't break up with us and he doesn't have a knocked up girlfriend. All he had to pay for was the surrogate he has."

"Actually, about that." I move out from behind the bar with my finger in the air and stand before the guys. I quickly put back on my glasses before continuing. "Remember that theory I was working on back in Purgatory about using parts of Lilith's essence and our sperm?"

"No!" They say in unison, the shock clear in their voices as they realize what I've accomplished.

"Yes. Lucy is carrying Lilith's and my child. Her essence with my biological makeup."

"So let me get this straight," Jessup says, turning to face me with his hands on his hips. "Adam betrayed Lilith and stabbed her with a God-blessed dagger and threw her to the seventh level of Hell. Then he somehow tricked us into believing it was her that tore out our hearts and told us to leave. L.A.M.B. rescued her, Anwen gave her a prophecy that said she needed to find us STAT, you two made up, and now we have less than 48 hours to make up with our homicidal ex-mate, that's not really our ex?"

"Yep," I enthusiastically nod.

"Great!" Jessup throws his arms up in the air.

I'm confused, shouldn't he be happy?

"She'll skin my beast and use me as a rug," Jessup says and then motions between Daniel and Matthew. "And your balls? She'll probably use them as paper weights and earrings. There's no possibility in all the levels of Hell that there's a way to make this up to her," he says and picks up the bottle of Everclear before he downs the rest of it. "She'll never forgive us for what she went through," he mutters, picking at his nails.

Oh yeah. They're fucked.

Visible shudders run through Matthew, and Daniel turns a shade whiter as Jessup's words sink in.

"I'm sorry I didn't believe you, Carl. We should have taken what you were saying seriously at the time," Matthew's voice cracks with remorse.

"We fucked up. Sorry, Steinbeck," Daniel grumbles.

"Yeah. We should have believed you when you were so

adamant about Lilith not doing that. We're sorry," Jessup's raspy voice says as he gives me a haunted look.

I nod, accepting their apologies and finally having my convictions recognized.

"Well, I'm glad we've all apologized to Steinbeck, but I'm still fucked. I like my balls, so I need a solution. It's no secret that I'm only with Lanna because she got knocked up and is carrying my heir. Other than that, I would have been over and done with her," Daniel admits, turning on his phone. His lip curls in disgust as he looks at his phone and sees a message ping from said woman.

I guess this is the best time to bring up what Lilith is working on in the lab. Granted it's up to the guys to decide if they will go through with it or not, but it will go a long way in getting back on Lilith's good side.

"There is one thing that you could do that would allow you to keep your balls," I say nonchalantly as I clean my glasses.

"Geez, man. Still killing us with the theatrics. You should have gone into drama instead of medicine," Daniel throws out.

Ignoring his comment, I continue, "Lilith was ecstatic that my theory actually worked and Lucy is bearing our child. She only wished that I would have done that for you all so your girlfriends were carrying hers as well."

The guys look away from me and won't catch my eyes. I sigh before I continue, "I didn't say that to make you feel bad —in fact—just the opposite. One of the reasons why Lilith stayed back is to work on something, in the hope that you will allow her to give your unborn children her essence so they can have a piece of her also."

"Is there really a chance that can work?" Matthew glances at me, hope shining through his hazel eyes.

My eyes roll before I give him a disbelieving look. "I can't believe you don't trust me or my word. How long have you known me?" I question.

"Too long," Jessup mumbles as he leans back in a chair, sipping from a bottle of jack.

When did he sit down?

I'm not sure he'll be able to stand up, let alone walk out of here, by the way he's drinking tonight.

"I heard that," I give him a pointed look.

"You were meant to," he states, grinning at me.

"So, our children could be a part of Lilith instead of the women we're with now?" Daniel asks. "Please, Fates, don't be pulling my leg on this one."

"Yes, they can. I could go on and explain how magical essence works if you'd like. It really is fascinating." I reach for a chair to get comfortable. "There's a wh—"

"No!" They all say in unison.

Talk about a mood killer.

"I probably speak for all of us, if by going off on the emotions alone, that we all want this," Matthew says, indicating the rest of the guys. "We haven't been happy in our relationships—"

"If you can call them that," Daniel interrupts. "It's not a relationship when we all know it was supposed to be a one night stand and since then, all the girls have been cheating on us and we're only putting up with it because of our kids." Daniel's eyes take on a reddish glow with his anger. I let out a sigh while I get a blood bag from the small fridge.

"Here," I say, handing him the O-negative from my work while biting my tongue from saying I told you so. It was one of the first things I told the guys when they were talking about hooking up with the girls. I told them they looked like bad news.

"I know we've been over this for months now, but I still don't understand how we even got them pregnant. We were all taking our potions. Plus, I thought once we found our mates, our dicks wouldn't work afterwards with anyone else but them. This should have been impossible," Matthew complains.

Jessup chuckles as he leans back on the two legs of his chair. "Need me to teach you about the birds and the bees, Mattie?"

"Put a cork in it, Jessie," Matthew snarks back and grabs his drink before he smiles back over at him, lightening the mood.

"Ah. Well, I might have an answer for that too," I hedge, waiting until all the guys give me their attention once again. "With the new information that Lilith presented, it's possible that our mate's bond was affected when she was stabbed. We still don't know what the effects were of the God-blessed dagger, but the fact that we could feel that fracture, I believe we were also affected by that. Or there could be something else that played into it that allowed your 'dicks' to perform for the task at hand."

"Fuuuck," Daniel groans.

"Yes. Fuck. The question, gentleman, is are you willing to let Lilith do this simple task and have it go a long way to bridging the gap between you all?"

I sit back and watch as my friends think about their options. But I've known them for centuries and I already know their answer.

CHAPTER 16

Girls just want to have fun

Lilith

Hearing the guys agreeing to my little plan last night turned me to mush. I'm surprised none of them noticed I was right outside, especially when Carl told them that they should be able to feel our bond. *Silly boys.* Let's just blame it on the alcohol. I watched my mates as they talked and picked on each other for the rest of the night, and a nostalgic feeling came over me. The only thing that kept me from walking in that door was the delicious idea of how I was planning on making them pay.

'*Yes, make them pay for all their sins,*' Grumpy says.

'*Burn the witch at the stake,*' Chew Toy squeaks. I internally roll my eyes to his suggestion.

'*Skin them alive and make a suit out of them,*' Rocks suggests.

I huff in annoyance for a few reasons 1) that I've done that before and it would be me repeating an all time favorite of mine, and 2) They've made a movie about someone copying me. *Can you believe that?* I know it's supposed to be flattering to copy my work, but it's downright sloppy, to say the least.

I ignore the pesky voices in my head as I continue to think back to my men. I'm in no way a saint, and even though they are my mates and apparently *"I"* was the one that told them to leave, they should have known better. How could one argument send them spiraling when we've spent eons together? I will deal with the issue of Adam somehow tricking them, but right now, I have bigger issues to deal with first. Either way, I am here now and I'm going to set things straight.

Adam is already in Hell and paying for his deeds, so all I need to do is set my men on the right track and everything will be perfect.

'Yes. Yes it will. But the mothers will still be in their lives, won't they?' Grumpy speaks up once again, voicing one of my fears.

This possession is slowly driving me mad. I can feel it. It's as if poison is slipping through my veins and insidiously spreading throughout my tissue, slowly decaying what's left of *me*. I'm afraid if I continue on this way, I'll soon not be able to tell if it's me or the Demons who control me. They are already voicing my own concerns. Will they be able to simply take over my life? Will anyone have any idea?

Chills race down my spine as that thought really sinks in. Fates, I hope that's not the case. Maybe that's why Anwen mentioned I needed to find my mates so soon. Maybe it's a damn side effect from being without my mates for so long that they're able to control so much of me. It's the only reason I can think of that would allow my blackouts and waking with no memory of what happened. Either way, it's a part of me that I have to fight until I can find a way to fix this.

'Or you can live with it,' Chew Toy gives me an option.

'It will just be like living with those women once they have those children,' Rocks chimes in.

As much as I want to disagree with him, he's not wrong. I wonder if I can just pay them off so they will sign over the children *I* should be having.

No! Just stick to the plan, Lilith.

I run my palms down the front of my yellow sundress to smooth it, and wave my hands, changing my boots into peek-a-boo sandals. With one last deep breath, I raise my fist to knock on the front door right as it opens and Daniel jerks at the sight of me. He's stunning in a pinstripe suit and one of his favorite pairs of shoes from Purgatory.

"Lilith!" His voice comes out in a husky whisper. As if he can't believe his own eyes. "It's true. You're back," he says as his shaky hand reaches for my face.

Faster than lightning his head snaps to the side with the crack of my palm. Just as fast, he grabs my hand and holds it gently as he slowly turns to face me once again. Heat flares in his yellow eyes as the tip of his tongue licks the blood from his busted lip.

"I don't care how Adam tricked you, there had to be signs you missed. Have you thought about your mistakes or what you're willing to do to pay for them?" I accuse but keep my all-knowing smirk on my face.

"Actually, yes. Last night after I stroked my cock and came to your memory, I thought about our so-called-argument. You knocked on the door and I let you in. And you were wearing a black dress instead of the one you picked out the night prior." His cocky smirk says it all. He's sorry, but he doesn't want to give in. It's our old cat-and-mouse game we used to play. He's always been the fire to my icy heart, and when we meet, we combust.

"First of all, I'm not known to change my clothes once I've set them out, and is that what I would do even if I didn't have my key with me?" I ask seductively.

"If I remember correctly, you would blow down the door

if you found it locked," he leans in, close enough for me to feel his breath on my lips.

I'm so tempted to claim his lips, but I do have morals...even though I like to blur the lines into gray. I'm here for something else.

I break his hold on my wrist, effectively making him stand back up. Hurt and disappointment reflect in his eyes as I don't easily forgive him. "So...There was a part of you that knew something was off that day, and yet you easily fell for the trap he set," I accuse.

"Don't start, Lilith. Can't you see that I've suffered enough without you? I could easily turn around and ask how Adam trapped you, but I won't. I'm all for burying the past and finding a way to do what's right." He reaches up and brushes the loose hair behind my ear and looks deeply into my eyes. My breath catches as I fight against the urge to lean into his palm and goosebumps run along my arms, my core heating with desire. "I am sorry that we failed you. That *I failed* you. I'm supposed to save and protect you, and instead, I took my anger and fled thinking you wanted nothing to do with me. And because of that, I tried to move on and every second has been pure torture without you, and now I'm stuck with..." He glances back at his house for a moment, and his eyebrows furrow in confusion as he glances at me.

Leaning back, his hand drops from my cheek as his eyes leisurely devour my outfit. "Well, I suppose you're here to find that out for yourself? Why are you here, Lilith?" he wonders, his eyes squinting in question.

I give him a mischievous smile as my hands glide up his muscular chest and under his lapels. "This is good quality. Italian. Brioni, if I'm not mistaken."

"Lilith," he bemoans, reaching for my hands. He brings them up to his lips and gives them a kiss before continuing. "What are you up to?"

"It's been a while since I've had a girls' day. I'm just here to have some fun," I admit, smiling and easily slipping past him and into the foyer of his home. "Hmm. Nice gig." The entry is completely empty of his personality, and it proves my theory that he's just putting up a façade and can't truly be himself. The real question is: is it because of the woman I can hear down the hall, or is it being on Earth in general?

"Lilith," Daniel growls, but I don't turn around as I continue my perusal. "I know your kind of fun. I can't have a blood bath in my home. Especially involving women that are pregnant and carrying our chil—"

My tail whips out and tightly wraps around his throat. I slowly turn to face him. My face is a careful mirage of patience when all I feel is Hellfire flowing through my veins.

'Kill him,' Rock hisses.

'He is worthless to us,' Chew Toy retorts.

'He's already betrayed you once, what's to stop him from doing it again?' Grumpy growls.

I blink away the red tint of my vision and see Daniel clawing at his neck as my tail is wrapped dangerously tight around his throat.

Shit.

"You would be wise not to remind me of that," I growl out, slowly releasing the pressure around his neck. "As of right now, I've decided to take another route instead of what you're insinuating." I give him a saucy wink and grin while my tail spins him around and swats him on the ass. "So go away, have a guys' day, and let me play with the girls." He takes a few steps out of the door and gives me a bewildered look over his shoulder as I snap my fingers, closing the door in his face.

Conjuring my purse into existence, I check to make sure the contents haven't broken and plaster a bright smile on my face as I waltz down the hall following the sound of voices. Laughter erupts in the room right before I sweep in like I own the place. Honestly—I do own this place—the women just don't know it yet. All I have to do is snap my fingers and Daniel would be at my feet worshipping me and asking what I needed. But I figure it's better this way.

The laughter abruptly stops as I walk into the living room and look around.

"Who the fuck are you, and what are you doing here?" A blonde girl dressed as a bad rendition of Nancy from *the Craft* tries to stand up and give me a dirty look.

"Oh! Didn't Lucy tell you? I'm Lilith, and I'm here to celebrate with you. It's been ages since I've had a girls' day." I beam her way as I watch them enjoy a fruit platter with virgin mimosas.

"That's Lilith. The woman I was telling you all about," whispers Lucy as I approach. "Hello, Lilith," she says to me with the fakest smile ever. I should know, I came up with the term.

"Hello, Lucy. How are you feeling? Carl gave me some stuff to bring over for you. Actually, for all of you," I say reaching into my bag, but pause to look at the women. "Oh, I'm sorry. I'm Lilith, and you all are?"

Not like I needed them to tell me since I've done my research last night and this morning.

'Nor do we care,' Grumpy growls.

'Right!' Chew Toy agrees.

"Not interested," the goth girl says.

I slowly look at her from under my lashes and she visibly gulps. She might not know I'm different, but her basic instinct knows subconsciously I'm *fucking* dangerous.

"I'm Layla," a blonde woman says while she gets up with a friendly smile. "Here, come join us." She grabs a chair and pulls it closer to her at the end, allowing me to sit. I smooth out my dress—abandoning the contents in my bag—as a waiter quickly brings me over a plate full of fruit with a croissant. I nod my thanks and bring my attention back to the women I came here to see.

"Thank you, Layla. That's sweet of you," I say before accepting the drink the server brings me next.

"As you already know, that's Layla, and Lucy. I'm Lily, and the grumpy one over there is Lanna." She points to the corresponding girls. After that, it's as if a dam opens up and we spend the next hour talking. They are a plethora of information, and I'm the sponge that sits back and soaks it all in. It turns out they've been friends since grade school and promised to always stay close. How their friendship worked was they would take turns doing what the other enjoyed doing. It's not until the girls start to remove their jewelry for the mani-pedis that something catches my eye.

Glancing between the women, I notice all of them wearing the same color of stone in their jewelry. The stones themselves are a pretty pink and yellow swirl encased in what looks like gold. If I didn't know better I would say they looked like Demstones. They were a rare combination of Brimstone and Star Rubies. They were known to hold powerful spells and were extremely hard to acquire.

"Those are lovely trinkets. Where did you get them?" I ask the group, and it's Layla who lights up.

"Ahh. That was my idea, I'm ashamed to say," she admits, color rushing to her cheeks as the other women laugh at her. "I have a thing for festivals and tarot card readings."

"So it was our turn to do what Layla wanted one weekend and sure enough, there was a Zodiac festival we'd never heard of, but she wanted to check it out," Lanna explains rolling her eyes and picking at her cuticles.

"Sue me," Layla replies with a chuckle. "Besides, you had fun if I remember correctly."

"We went into the fortune teller's tent and as soon as we walked in, we were greeted by this drop-dead gorgeous woman. I mean I'm bi and all, but I was about to drop down on one knee and propose right then and there," Lily confesses with a blush when we make eye contact.

"I just remember her hypnotic gray eyes and how they seemed to suck you in when she looked at you," Lanna recounts. She points to the nail polish she wants while Layla picks back up the story.

"I know with most fortune-tellers, they have you pay and they do your fortune one at a time, but this woman insisted that all four of us stay and said she saw something special in us." Layla grabs her ankle bracelet and hands it to me. "She actually gave us these to wear for good luck. She said we were destined to have them and they would lead us to our true loves. That we would find them in a group of friends that were closer than blood. Our destiny was bigger than what we could ever know." Her voice trails off as her eyes look off in the distance.

As soon as the bracelet makes contact with my skin, red filters across my vision for a split second before the room goes dark.

CHAPTER 17
Bloody Departed

Lilith

D*rip. Drip. Drip. Drip.* The constant dripping of liquid landing on my cheek arouses me from another blackout. Without moving, I slowly take in and catalog my surroundings. There's a hard floor underneath me and I'm lying in something wet. Did I fall in the pedicure tub? That would be disgusting if not embarrassing in front of the women.

During my search for my mates, I found out the hard way that it takes a few minutes to regain full control of my body after a blackout. The first time I tried to stand, I ended up rolling down a hillside and almost drowned in a lake. Thankfully, I was able to move my wings sufficiently to block the water long enough to gain proper control.

Opening my eyes, I find myself plastered to the hardwood floor and facing Daniel's hallway to the foyer. I feel my tail swish back and forth in irritation, and my eyes go wide in panic.

Fuck! I'm naked and in my Demon form.

What if the girls see me like this? They can't know I'm a fucking Demon! How in the hell am I going to explain that?

'Haha. You don't need to worry about that anymore.' Chew Toy giggles, and lead drops in my stomach.

'What did you do?' My inner voice comes out an octave higher than normal in my panic.

'Now where's the fun in that?' Chew Toy replies.

I will my arms to move, but it's my wings that respond. They shift me a little bit to the point that I can see back towards the area where I had been sitting and what I see makes me gasp.

There's a trail of blood from me to the body in front of my chair. I can tell from here that it's one of the technicians that was working to give us a mani-pedi, but that's all I can see from here.

What happened?

'Do you like our handy work?' Grumpy asks like a child looking for praise from their parents. *'I really can't take all the credit of course. You did all the heavy work, and Rocks had the idea.'*

Fear propels me and I pull myself up on wobbly legs as red tissue lands down at my bare feet.

Plop.

I've seen my fair share of livers laying severed before me. Most of them I've pulled out with my bare hands, but I've done that in my torture rooms, not in my mate's house. Looking up, I see one of the technicians disemboweled and strung up between the two chandeliers. If it wasn't for where I was and the circumstances, I could almost take in the beauty of it all. Their intestines are strung out along the lights as if they were hung up for Christmas morning—all twenty-five feet of them.

My feet make wet slurping noises while I slowly make my way through the destruction of the room. A moan pulls my attention to behind the chair where I spot Layla's face scrunched up in pain.

"Layla!" I rush to her side, not caring what I look like, only to see her holding her abdomen and gasping for air.

"Help," she mouths and then coughs, blood spewing out of her mouth.

I hear another moan and realize it came from Lily who is behind her. With a quick glance, I note she's not doing much better. Blood is seeping from her lower leg in an alarming amount. I know enough that if we don't stop the bleeding, she will bleed out.

"Call 911," Lily mumbles and passes out.

Call? What does she mean by call? Shit? I glance behind me looking for a pad of paper and a pen and all I see on the stand is a cell phone.

Oh, call!

Well, fuck. Carl had tried to show me his phone last night, but I told him it would probably take me forever to get used to it. He had even bought me my very own this morning, but I left it at his house, saying there was no way I would need it. Against my protests, he showed me how to call and text him, but I was more interested in making up for lost time in other ways.

Reaching for her phone, I click a few buttons, hoping that she has Carl's name and number stored in her phone. My shoulders slump as tears build up in relief at seeing his name in her short contact list. Leaving bloody fingerprints behind, I click call and wait with baited breath for his voice to come over the phone.

"Lily? What do—"

"Carl! Help! The girls...something's wrong. I think they're dying. Hurry, please!" I ramble out as fast as I can. Thankfully, I had told him my plan to come and crash the girls' party today and give them my essence. According to my calculations, it should bypass the women and search for my mate's DNA. Once found, it will erase the human DNA from the babies and boost the supernatural strand with my essence in order to make the children stronger.

My heart's beating out of my chest as I stand up, looking around for the other two and find them on the other side of the room by the buffet table, unconscious.

"Lilith, we'll be there in two minutes. We aren't far," Carl assures me, his tone coming across calm but rushed. I can hear him running on the other end. As he runs, my brain finally decides to kick in, and I conjure up a long dress and immediately drop the phone to rip off the bottom. Rushing back to Lily, I make a tourniquet around her thigh to try and stop the bleeding, and that's when I hear the roar of Jessup's bear right before the front door is busted off the hinges.

"Lilith, where are they?" Carl yells.

"Here!" I yell back and I check for Lily's pulse. It's so weak.

Footsteps pound down the hall until I see Daniel, Matthew, Carl, and Jessup—who is still in his bear form—slide into the room. Multiple displays of shock, horror, and anger dot their faces.

"What the fuck, Lilith. I said no bloodbaths. What is—"

"Where are they?" Carl says, cutting off Daniel and getting down to saving lives. It's one of the things I love about him. He's always put duty before himself, taking care of others and doing the best that he can.

"I don't know what happened, honestly. I just put a tourniquet on Lily and her pulse is weak. Layla is coughing up blood. Lanna and Lucy are unconscious on the other side of the room. I don't know what to do. Help!" I look around at my once lovers and beg them to believe me, but all I see is disbelief, uncertainty, and hatred.

Carl steps up and barks orders which thankfully takes the heat off of me for the moment.

"Jessup, shift! I need hands and you've had basic medical training. I need stats on the girls. I need heart rates, any injuries that you see and if they tell you anything, write it down." Jessup nods and quickly shifts before he runs over to Lucy as my heart breaks.

Just as I found them and was going to win them back, this happened.

"Matthew, I need you to get your healing potions from your house, all of them!" Mattie nods and rushes out of the house without another look in my direction.

"Daniel, you're my runner, since you're the fastest. I need my medical supplies brought here. They are labeled in the back room of my office, along the back wall. Plus, I need the ultrasound machine."

"Ok, I'll be right back," he confirms, and he glares at me before flying out of the room with his Vampire speed.

"Lilith, I need you to get a notebook and pen for Jessup. Then I need you to bring me all the towels and blankets that you can find." Without a word, I nod and rush out of the room. I had seen an office to the left when I first walked into the house, so that's where I head, leaving bloody footprints in my wake.

'Isn't this exciting?' Chew Toy exclaims.

'It's definitely the most fun I've had in a century. I've never even been to Earth,' Rocks admits.

Keep talking fuckers.

They're only giving me ammunition to rip them apart when I get my hands on them. Because believe me, if they've permanently ruined my chance of getting my mates back, there is no place in all the planes of existence that will keep them safe. Even inside me.

With a notebook and pen that I find on the desk, I race

back to Jessup where he's already crouched over Lucy with a pinched expression. He grabs the items from me without looking up and starts jotting down his notes. Daniel has been busy in the short amount of time it has taken me to find the items because there's already an ultrasound machine in the room, along with a few medical supplies that Carl is using.

"Lilith! The towels are in the two bathrooms upstairs and in the laundry room next to the kitchen!" Daniel yells at me as he drops a metal case by Carl's feet before rushing out the door again.

I make several trips with armloads of towels when Matthew passes me in the hallway with his own load of vials.

"Were you really that jealous of them?" he asks, not slowing down his pace and forcing me to catch up.

"It wasn't me, Mattie. You have to believe me," I plead. Tears burn in my eyes as he squints at me, reading my emotions. That was often a skill I relied on that helped me in the past, but I'm not sure what he'll pick up now that I'm possessed.

"We'll talk later."

That's all he says as he runs flat out into the room and helps Carl to prep Layla. From what I've been catching, the women are in bad shape and it doesn't look like they will make it.

I grab the last of the towels and a few bowls from the laundry room and bring them back but stop right outside of the door frame as I hear Jessup ask, "But can we even trust her?"

It's as if my heart is ripped out of my bleeding chest and acid is poured over the open sores of my rotten organ. I fight back the sharp inhale, knowing that they will hear me this close, and I grit my teeth instead. Fire courses through me as anger rises.

'*Ahh. Poor Lilith. Her mates can't trust her anymore,*' Chew Toy mocks.

'*Such a shame, really. Just imagine what they will say,*' Rocks says.

'*The most powerful Demon in all the realms, and her own* harem *doesn't want her, even when she came to them crawling on her belly.*' Grumpy chuckles. '*Because that's what you did. You went crawling to them when they were already in other relationships.*'

NO!

Shaking my head, I push their thoughts away and walk into the room with my head held high.

"If I wanted them dead, Jessup, I wouldn't have called for help," I call out to him and raise an eyebrow in his direction. We stare at each other without saying another word. I know what I'm doing, I'm challenging an Alpha and my mate, and it can be taken as a faux pas outside of the bedroom, but I want him to know how serious I am. He opens his mouth to say something but before he does, I break eye contact and walk over to Carl who's putting on sterile gloves.

"What can I do to help?" My voice is laced with worry.

Before he can reply, a monitor goes off and then another and another until all four of them are pinging. Carl's eyes go wide as Jessup runs to the first monitor and reads off the stats to him. It's pure chaos as the guys start yelling back and forth numbers and medical jargon that I'm oblivious to. I pick up a few words while I stand there dumbly and think of ways that I can help, but my specialty doesn't involve medical training at all. I loved spells, torture, fashion, and teaching. I'm completely hopeless here.

This is all my fault. Don't get me wrong, I'm all for torturing souls and often find myself in bloodlust while doing it, but I draw a line when it comes to children. I would have never attacked these women. If it wasn't for me wanting or needing—according to Anwen—my men back, then these women wouldn't be fighting for their lives right now, instead they would be getting their nails done, eating, and enjoying each other's company. I was the imposter here.

Shouts erupt, pulling me from my musing to see Layla take her last breath.

Oh no!

Her heart monitor flat lines and I watch as another monitor that's set up next to her starts to drop. Soon enough it becomes clear what I'm seeing as Carl quickly takes a scalpel and cuts into Layla's abdominal wall, separating her muscles to reach her uterus.

Her baby!

"We're losing him," Carl says, cutting into her corpse to deliver her baby early. I think the girls were saying they were around seven months pregnant. Can children survive outside of the uterus that far along?

I try to think of anything that might be able to help in this situation when I hear the sounds of the other guys shouting for help. Looking up, I notice all of the other monitors start to drop. Before I can do anything else, Carl hands me a big fluffy towel with a bloody child squirming about and says, "Save him." He runs over to help Jessup who's leaning over and performing CPR on Lily.

The child in my arms doesn't look like the babies I've seen before. This one is more like an alien with fuzz all over it while it squirms and barely makes a sound. It's all pale skin and bones and its eyes are still shut. In the simplest terms he looks like a twisted water dragon, like a Leviathan. I take a moment to look at it and I notice his lungs slowing down as he fights to take in air, the bluish tinge growing more pronounced on its face.

Carl said to save him. Did he mean for me to use my potion? Mix my DNA with his? It is worth a shot. Conjuring my purse to me, I lean down to open it when I feel the tell-tale signs of the Demons trying to push me back. My sight goes to pinpoints as I try to battle my way through it.

No! I can't allow myself to fail. This child needs me.

Something brushes against my cheek and I feel the Demons retreat. Looking down, I see the tiny little fingers of the child in my arms reaching for my face as his body struggles.

Did he just save me?

Not letting the moment pass me by, I quickly reach into my purse and pop the cork on the small vial of my essence I was going to give the women. I pour out the small vial over the child, and watch as it seeps into his skin. The change is instant as his bright hazel eyes peer up at me and his lungs take in a breath without fighting, and then he proceeds to let out a scream.

Eek!

What kind of devil child is this? Matthew runs over to me and proceeds to take the child from me, shushing him and talking in some type of language I'll definitely have to learn.

"Lilith!" Jessup calls. Turning to face him, I see him holding a bundle in his arms as well and it makes my heart melt. "Can you help save him?" his voice catches as he asks for help.

I quickly grab the rest of the vials I had brought and spend the next hour, saving the pieces of my harem's heart.

CHAPTER 18
Not Quite Right

Matthew

I can't believe Lilith is really here. I mean I listened to everything that Carl said last night, but to see her sitting here in front of us, it's unreal. And if I'm reading the room correctly, I'm not the only one. The past four hours have been a blur with emotions ranging from joy to devastation, anger, to remorse. Nothing has been off the table in the range of the unbelievable.

For instance, I never thought Lilith would ever attack pregnant women. She's always enjoyed torturing souls and the Demons that needed to be put in their place, but I had thought children were off limits.

She did step up and help though.

While our sons were on the brink of death, she held them close and applied her essence which in turn saved their lives, according to Steinbeck. He checked them over before he joined us in cleaning up the aftermath of Lilith's destruction. While we cleaned and took care of the issue at hand, we allowed Lilith to take care of the children, under our watchful eyes of course. I watched as she hummed while she cleaned, dressed, and even named our children. Leviathan, Knox, Ryker, and Ezekiel.

She conjured up matching cribs with their names engraved on them, and they are currently resting peacefully at her side as I sit across from her. I'm not going to lie, seeing her like this does something to me. I like seeing her maternal side come out. I just wish it hadn't started with the destruction of so many lives.

After cleaning up the room and disposing of the bodies, we needed a story to cover our tracks, and that's where Daniel came in. He had some powerful friends high up on the political food chain that could easily get us out of trouble. We're no strangers to hiding bodies, but with Earth's politics, we needed to work around a few obstacles, like a paper trail.

"Well, my friend is going to take care of the report for us. Thankfully the girls don't have any immediate family," Daniel says with a somber look while walking through the living room to join us.

Well since that's done, it looks like the only problem we now face is the woman sitting in front of us.

I'm torn as I look back at Lilith. She looks so serene as she glances down at her son, Ryker. Lilith is the reason my son, Leviathan, is alive right now, yet he was in that position because of her to begin with.

"Tell me again, what happened?" Jessup says, pinching the bridge of his nose before his eyes soften as he takes in his son lying in his crib.

Lilith's jaw clenches in frustration, and I feel her desperation to have us believe her. She takes in a deep breath before placing her hands into her lap and looks at our group.

"I came here only to get to know the women and to give them my essence, Jessup. I didn't plan on anything else to happen besides that," she tells him. "Please, you have to believe me. I didn't do it. I know hurting them would only hurt you in the long run, and I came here to get you back. I miss you all and I love you."

I feel her innocence at the forefront of her mind, but there's something deeper there...something like *satisfaction*? Why would there be satisfaction as an undercurrent to this situation?

"Everything was going well, until I saw all of their matching jewelry and I asked about it." She turns to Carl to ask, "Why didn't you tell me they were all wearing Demstones?"

"What?" Carl startles. "Where did you see those?"

"The girls all had matching stones that they received from a fortune teller..." she trails off as she takes in our faces.

How did we not know about this? I mean, besides the one night stand I had, which I was somewhat tipsy during, I don't pay much attention to human jewelry. *Why would I?*

"Could that have been what allowed us to 'perform' that night?" Daniel asks the group.

"It's possible, depending on what spells were layered in the stones," Carl replies.

Shit! Didn't Layla mention something about how close the girls were that they even had matching jewels? Is that what they were talking about? Could that be why we all decided to hook up with them? Were we somehow compelled or spelled? And if that was true, why wasn't Carl affected by it?

"They told me a story about how a fortune teller gave them matching jewelry—which was the Demstones—and told them where to find you all and how you would be their true loves. When Layla handed me her stone, I blacked out. I awoke to find...my handiwork. Please!" She chokes a sob back as she drops to her knees from her chair. "Don't cut me out because of something I couldn't control. At least let me work my way back into your lives," she pleads once again and tears start to stream down her cheeks.

I can feel how desperately she loves us and wants us back. It's as if she's pulling at my heart with her bare hand and asking for me to hug her. I want to go to her and wrap her in my arms and tell her everything will be okay, but I also sense those fragments of deep-rooted feelings that are telling me she's taking sick pleasure in this.

"At least don't deny me my children. I know I wasn't the one that carried and birthed them, but without my essence, they would have perished too. I want to have the chance to love and cherish them like a mother would. Please... d-don't keep them from me. At least allow me that while I try to earn your forgiveness and work my way back into your arms."

Jessup, Daniel, and Carl give me pointed looks. Well, Carl looks at me and nods—his mind made up—before going to Lilith and pulling her into a hug and kissing her gently.

"You never had to ask for my forgiveness. I will always be your mate, your love, and anything else you need me to be, my dear." He steps behind her and wraps his arms around her waist to face us. She leans into his embrace for a moment before turning her hopeful gaze onto the rest of the group.

"What do you say?" Daniel questions, his tone flat as he sits motionless in his chair.

Daniel might be sitting there like a statue, but his emotions are flying around like a hurricane. Anger, despair, amusement, happiness, but overall, he just feels confusion. Danny has never been easy for me to read, but what I do pick up is that he's scared to make the call. Which direction is right in this instance? Allowing Lilith back into our life and dismiss what all has happened or close her out entirely? Secretly, he's hoping that I make the call in this case.

I'm torn. I sit here a broken man. Even though a part of me believes what Lilith is saying to be true, I can't fully trust her. Yes, it's true I didn't love my girlfriend the way I felt for my mate before me, but the fact is, Lilith crossed a line. She put my own child in danger, and that's something she should have been able to fight against for him.

For me.

Her love.

Her mate.

Shouldn't she have been able to fight that spell? Lilith, the original Demon?

I take a moment to assess the room, and what I find shocks me for a moment while I process the feelings I'm picking up.

Jessup shifts in his seat, showing his annoyance, and I focus in on his hot temper. He's practically screaming his emotions, not even trying to shield himself. Mate or not, he's been hurting without her for years, and it seems she will need to do some begging of her own if she wants back onto his good graces. "I feel her innocence, that I won't deny, but there's a small part within her that is satisfied by this outcome." I watch as Lilith's face falls slightly, yet the emotions I pick up on are horror and happiness. *What is going on with that?*

"She believes down in her soul that she didn't do this. But the facts are, she is the only survivor of this massacre besides our children," I point out regrettably.

I won't take away my child from her, but like she was going to make us earn her forgiveness for everything we did, I'm going to make her work for my forgiveness. I'm not going to make it easy for her. I have to make her fight for me and my child if she wants to stay in our lives.

Daniel turns to deliver his verdict to Lilith but before he does, one of the children—Ezekiel—starts fussing and Lilith swoops down to pick him up, cradling him to her. He immediately quiets down as she starts rocking him. While Daniel watches her closely, I add one other thing they don't know. "Our boys are happy with her," I state.

Everyone seems to freeze. The only sound is Lilith's gasp and Ezekiel's small sounds.

"What did you say?" Jessup growls, staring at me as if I'm his next target.

"Our boys. They're projecting, and not feelings about us, but about Lilith," I simply answer, not knowing how to explain it further.

"How can that be?" Daniel asks on a whisper.

"Maybe when Lilith gave them her essence, it changed them in more ways than one," Steinbeck concludes, peering over Lilith's shoulder at the baby. "There's only one way to find out."

"What's that, my prince?" Lilith murmurs quietly to not disturb the sleeping boy.

"Wait and see."

CHAPTER 19
I got no strings on me

Adam

Time moves differently for those that have constantly suffered. We don't watch the clock or count days. Instead, we are reduced to celebrating the little victories no one else deems important. Like one extra soul that you got to join the cause, taking one for the team, or having your skin grow back after being flayed off for sick amusement.

Fuck Bez and his love for cutting and melting my skin off as slow as fucking possible. No wonder he and Lilith are best friends. They each take sick pleasure in the demented ways of torture and have the blackest hearts in Hell. To this day, I swear, she has no soul.

I've spent the last—I don't know how many hours—in that sick fuck's presence. Who knew that the same cage I threw Lilith in would be a reprieve from the Vengeance Demon's care? The dark room smells of piss and blood, *my bodily fluids,* yet I couldn't care less. My skin has finally stopped the insufferable itching. It's been slowly regrowing over the past few hours, and the stages, I dare say, are not comfortable to deal with. First is the fire stage as the cells ignite and start to repair. Second is the lightning as the nerves regrow. Every layer of skin I can feel thanks to Lilith and a curse she threw my way eons ago when she learned I couldn't die. Even the soothing part—which I'll never feel again because my ex-wife is soulless—should feel like cool water running over my skin, leaving it feeling refreshed. Before, growing back my skin or rejuvenating any part of my body was quick and painless, but now it's a slow and painful experience that I have to relive constantly.

The process is a long one, but I'll happily lay here as long as one of L.A.M.B. doesn't come for me again. Grinding metal pulls me from my musings and I glance up in a panic thinking that L.A.M.B. is coming for another round of torture. A glow penetrates the darkness and I can see a dark robe pulled over a creature's head as the light moves deeper within the room and the door closes, leaving us alone. The figure stops in front of the cage and places the torch in a holder on the wall.

"My my my, how the mighty have fallen," a familiar voice chuckles. As the hood falls back, I take in the presence before me. Blond hair just a little bit longer than my own is tousled from the hood being thrown back. Tan skin seems to glow where it's highlighted from the light of the torch on the wall. There's a light scruff along the man's chiseled jaw and above it is a smirk on his full lips. No doubt he's enjoying the predicament of me lying in my own filth. "Still think it was a good idea to gloat about your victory over Lilith?" His familiar gray eyes sparkle with mirth as I glare up at my identical twin.

The world believes it's myself and Eve or even Lilith that was created first—but really—it was Aaron and myself. We squabbled and fought over the simplest things until God—in his all mighty fuckery—told us to separate to the far sides of the Garden of Life. Shortly after, I was given Lilith, and she rocked my world. She changed me in more ways than one.

The most notable was when I found myself attacked by a lion and I was dying. I prayed to the bastard that gave me life, and all he said is that it was the way of the land. As I laid there under the tree, my only wish was that I could heal myself, and to my surprise and God's...I did. By the time I found my way back to Lilith, God was smiting her to Hell and she happily left with a horde of fallen angels. Before she left, at some point she apparently had slept with me again, not knowing it was Aaron, and had changed him also.

God created Eve for us to share, and between you and me, I would have had a better lay if I fucked a fish. Aaron and I took turns sharing her without her even realizing it, until she fucked us over and allowed Lucifer to trick her. Eve wasn't the brightest, and it wasn't until God kicked us out of the Garden of Life that Aaron and I even knew we were different beyond our unintended immortality.

When we found ourselves cast out of the garden, we found that we could easily hide when we needed to. It started off small, blending in with the foliage around the trees and the grass surrounding us. It wasn't until we met other humans that we started to document their differences. Then one morning a man—that I didn't know—walked into my house and made himself at home.

It took Aaron explaining intimate things about me before I believed it was him, and I had to take him down to the lake for him to believe that he didn't look like himself. We spent ages learning and defining our skills, always staying close, allowing one to play as Adam and the other to pose as another inconspicuous person. This assignment just so happened that I was playing myself.

"I did what I had to do," I grunt and shift over to the bars. "What *we* planned, remember?" I grasp the bars and pull myself up to a sitting position and look up at my brother. "Now get me out of here!"

"How did you even get in there in the first place?" Aaron says.

"L.A.M.B. happened. They freed our ex and she came for her pound of flesh. How else do you think she got out?" I growl with frustration. My entire body shakes with anger as I watch him look at me with pity. I don't want pity.

I want out of this cage.

I want to be free.

I want revenge.

Ever since I slept with the devil, all puns included, I've been cursed.

"Well, that's unfortunate," he says and sits down in front of me like he's waiting to be served lunch.

What the fuck is he thinking?

"What the fuck are you doing? Get me out of here, Aaron," I seeth. "Obviously, my part of the plan worked, so get me out of here so we can fix your part of it."

All he does is scoff and smirks at me before I lose it and start to rant.

"How do you know your part of the plan even worked?" he questions, slanting an eyebrow at me.

I slump against the cage, the hard bars digging into my back as I take in a breath to regain my strength. "Because, dearest brother, I coated the God-blessed dagger with angel dust and performed the task of helping the Demons cross over myself." I glance over and take pleasure in seeing Aaron's face go slack in shock. I went above and beyond in gaining angel dust and taking the extra steps to make sure our ex was out of the picture, so this bastard better let me out.

"How the—nevermind. I don't want to know how you got the dust. I must say I'm impressed," he admits. Although for saying he's impressed, he sure doesn't look like it as he quickly hides a smirk. "Who did you put inside her? Hopefully, it was someone that can do the job."

Now it's my turn to smirk. "Pyro, Genesis, and Tempus."

"Wait...as in the children of Asmodeus—the Demon prince of lust?" Aaron questions, his eyes widening slightly in the glow of the light.

"Now who's the better twin? I fucked Lilith first *and* got her possessed by the prince's children," I say with pride.

"But look where you're at," Aaron points out as he stands, making his point. "You're there and I'm here, free as a bird."

"That might be the case, but I completed my task. You, on the other hand, haven't," I smirk.

The silence between us is almost deafening as I watch him pull out a bottle of liquid from his robe. The liquid sizzles as it breaks the lock on my cage and he opens the door so I can shakily crawl out of my prison. I swallow the grunts as I slowly stand and stretch out to my full height but quickly lean against the cage for support.

All my very supportive brother does is smirk at me, taking joy at my misery, like usual.

"It's not at all funny, Aaron. I used up all my energy regrowing my fucking skin after L.A.M.B. had some fun with me, so I need to rest before I'll be of any use," I say with a sneer. He mimics my expression when I mention Lilith's besties, or pets, but other than that the twinkle in his eyes doesn't leave. Having enough of his brand of torture, I push for the news that he's holding.

Aaron starts rocking on his feet like he's a toddler for a moment and I snap. "Why are you so happy?" I hiss, throwing my arms in the air. "We have to figure out how to pull this off since you failed. You were supposed to capture Lilwen, not kill her! You completely fucked this up."

"I did?" he questions and right before my eyes, I watch his body shift with ease—nothing like our normal skinwalker abilities. There's actually nothing normal about our abilities. When Aaron and I were thrown out of the Garden of Life with Eve, she became a banshee, a breed of her own that could see death coming and mourned it. Aaron and I became what we called skinwalkers. We are the only ones in existence. We can change our forms to duplicate another, but it's quite painful and drains us of energy quickly. I watch as his eyes change from swirling gray eyes to one of a pentagram and swirling yellow.

I gasp as I take in the unique eyes that the Fates are known to have, yet we've never been close enough to see in person. "How? I thought she was found dead. Won't her power transfer to someone else to take her place?" I whisper in awe.

The tinkling of Aaron's laughter catches me off guard for a moment as I'm not expecting such an angelic sound to come out of my satanic brother.

"She *is* dead, but it won't be transferring to anyone because I have it, or technically—drained it," he states matter-of-factly.

Cocking my head, I glance at my brother's new image, "So, what am I supposed to call you by now? He? She? It?" I give him a knowing look. I know he hasn't thought all of this out.

"They?" He shrugs and pulls a small vial from his pocket and holds it out for me to take. "And I found a way for us to speed up our recovery time also."

"How?" I ask, taking the vial filled with a dark liquid and sounding like a broken record.

"Remember the Sulks?" they asks, and my eyes go wide at the mention of the death strip. Why would they mention that? It used to be a portal to Earth that went rogue back in the day, and it stopped us from traveling through it centuries ago.

"Y-Yeah," I hesitate and look down at the vial in my hand.

"Well, I found a way to use it to siphon magic from others to make us stronger," they admits. "Now drink your hard-earned Sulks offering."

I look down at the vial of black liquid.

It must have been a tainted soul that they drained to get this magic for me.

Popping the top, I inhale the burned parchment and black licorice smell. *Blood Magic.* It reminds me of *home* and I down the essence that calls to me. Warmth floods my body, heating me up from the inside, and I feel energy surge through me.

"Good, huh?" they asks and quickly morphs back into his normal form, making it look easy. I'm somewhat envious, but I know it's for a greater cause, so I'll try and stave off my jealousy.

"Do I even want to know how long I've been in there?" I ask once I loosen up my limbs.

"At least a day, in the seventh level of Hell time," Aaron shrugs like it's no big deal.

I roll my eyes and decide against decking him. "You couldn't get me out of here sooner?" I ask, pushing past him and heading towards the door.

"Why? What's the rush?"

How he wasn't the twin that got skinned alive, I'll never know.

"Lilith! She's out there trying to get her mates back and—"

"Well, let's call them back and don't give them the time to rekindle, shall we," he says, easily morphing into his Fate persona again, and I feel my spirits lift for the first time since we came up with this plan.

Epilogue

Aaron

It's been a long time since I've been down to the second level of Hell and the first time since we started this alliance. The succubus in front of me gives an extra sway of her hips, her tail flinging out and brushing my cock, rousing it from its slumber. She's gorgeous, curves in all the right places, small onyx horns, heart-shaped tail, and big doe eyes. My weakness. She's definitely a minx, and if it wasn't a death sentence to keep my partner waiting, I would bend her against the wall and take her right now. She glances over her shoulder and gives me a seductive smile as we approach the double doors.

"Maybe once you're done with your appointment, you'll make one with me?" She smiles and gazes up at me as she passes. I know, the face I wear is a looker. It's been one of my favorites since the beginning of time—with a few tweaks here or there—so it's one that I consider my own. Black curly hair, silver eyes, and a tanned muscular body.

"Come find me and I will," I flirt and adjust myself before walking through the doors.

The cavernous room is dark except for the soft glow of white and red candles sporadically placed around the room. The Prince of Lust loves the ambience of the red sheen in his fuck room. He once told me, he enjoyed the idea of his guest wondering if it was just the light or blood that coated his walls. Today, it's blood by the smell of it. I can make out a small sitting area off to the right where a plate of food sits along with pillows that line the hard floor. In the back right corner— where moans are coming from—are a couple of women enjoying each other's flesh on a bed of pillows. In the back left corner is a sex table with various toys lining the wall. Shadows dance and cover the left side of the room, where I can only assume is my host.

"Ah! Aaron. Nice of you to join me. Come. Tell me some good news." A new flicker of light appears above me as Asmodeus walks out from the shadows and motions for me to follow him.

I forgot how big he was. Eight feet tall, four horns, two facing the front as two facing the back. I've seen human pictures that tried to depict the Demon with multiple heads of beasts, but that's probably the most ridiculous thing I've ever seen. Who has ever heard of a lust Demon with heads of beasts? Try a Demon with multiple cocks? As the Prince of Lust, he can control how many he has at a time. Currently he's sporting two, and it looks like I was interrupting something as we pass two more female Demons pleasing each other that I somehow missed.

We sit down on plush pillows that are scattered around the sitting area and as soon as he gets comfortable, the females scurry over to us, each taking one of his cocks into their mouth.

Okay then!

If I stay in his presence much longer, I might be using his succubus for more than a quick lay.

Tearing my eyes from them, I look back up at one of the most cunning Demons I know. Asmodeus gives me a knowing smile, and I'm sure he's picking up on the lust that's coming from me.

"The seeds have been planted and they have taken root. Not long now and you will have your biggest obstacle out of your way," I tell him.

"Good. Good." He smiles.

R oad to Salvation will be the 4th book in the Series!
  *Road to Salvation: Purgatory Prep Academy Book four, coming soon.

Darkest Desires Drink & Food List

(Here's a list of Drinks and Food that my Alpha and I came up with one night of brain storming. We might have gotten carried away)

Drinks:

Purple Peen

Jizz Wiz

Pussy Destroyer

Double Decker Pecker

Pink Pecker Eater

Ball Buster

Hersey Nipple Suckers (shots)

Fuzzy Clam Jam

Smoky Pokey Cumshots

Tatwaffe Cum Guzzler

Peek a Boo Pucker Shots

FaeFire Farts

Pretty pussy Pounders

Pixie Bubble Butts

Dirty Pimp Pump

Food:

- Plenty of penis tarts
- Cotton candy penis sticks
- Boomballstic brownies
- Cuntalicious tacos
- Orgasmic anal apples
- Peengasmic pickles
- Queen cuntasaurus (sour treat)
- Shaggy curtain flapjacks
- Perky titty flaps
- Cream de la cocks
- Hellish Firecrotch Nachos
- Chilic Con Cum Nachos
- Funnel Cocks w/ twisted nut butter

Looking for More

First of all I want to say thank you, the reader, for picking up this book and giving me the chance to create a world for you to escape into. I was a little nervous about writing Lilith's story since it was a little darker than what I normally write, but it was one that needed to be told.

I hope you enjoyed a sneak peak into her life before the boys were born and hopefully understand what caused her to act the way she's been in the first book of the series.

I would love to hear your thoughts on the series so far or even on this book, if this is the first that you've read of the series. It would mean the world to me if you could leave a review wherever you bought the book.

Want more of the Purgatory gang?

Preorder Book 4

Road to Salvation

Or start the series

Road to Redemption

Thank you!

There are always so many people to say thank you too, so let's get started.

Jillian, my Alpha and my ride or die! Thank you for being there every step of the way in this process and stepping up when I needed it! I can't wait to see what we come up with next!

Cassie Hurst, my bossy minion and content editor. I'm glad we didn't lose our minds with this book. I really don't know what I would do without you. Please don't leave me, ever! Thank you for sticking with me.

Hope Brown, my book whisperer and graphic wizard. You bring my books to life! Thank you for being my PA and keeping me from jumping off the edge.

Kellie, thank you for your love of the English word and editing this beauty.

Leanne, you killed it with this cover! I can't wait to see what else you do for this series! You are amazing, thank you!

And of course, my betas. Bonnie (Stab a bish) Nyas, Lin (book dragon) Lasky, Naedrax (Horror queen) Rb, Isabealla (Sweet Izzy) Mackenzie, Becca (Cheerleader) Sabala, Tanya (Eagle eye) Courtney, and Jacquie (Thirsty) Stolz. You girls keep me motivated and bring me so much joy. I love you all.

My ARC team are the best type of hype group. Always ready to go at a drop of the hat. Getting the first look at the books, reviewing and letting me know if I've made a mistake. Thank you so much for being my last stand and first on the front line.

I also want to thank Kira Roman for sprinting with me to get this book out. Of course, Brady Möller, Rosa Lee, November Sweets, Lexie Winston, have once again been by my side with their support and I love you all for it.

Finally to my Aunt Patty, mom and sister. You guys are my constant support and I thank you for checking up on me and making sure I don't get buried behind the computer screen. Once again my Kaeden James is the MVP in pushing me to write more books. Thank you for taking the bullet and giving me time to write during our hectic schedule. I love you, little man.

www.ingramcontent.com/pod-product-compliance
Lightning Source LLC
Chambersburg PA
CBHW051837170626
46807CB00003B/1223